DE'LURE PUBLICATIONS

De'Lure Shorts & Poems II

TEN ORIGINAL SHORT STORIES & POEMS

De'Lure Shorts

& Poems

2

De'Lure

De'Lure Shorts 2

De'Lure Shorts & Poems 2

10 Original Short
Stories and Poems All
Rights Reserved.

Copyright ©
2016
De'Lure v2.0
r1.0

Cover Image by Edifyin Graphics

De'Lure Publishing

PRINTED IN THE UNITED STATES OF AMERICA

Author Quotes

"Always remember that the trouble in your past is already done and it never changes... so in turn never be discouraged when fighting a battle that you've already fought so many times before, look instead to your inevitable future."

De'Lure

"I will die a dreamer... A dreamer with the heart and the talent to realize their dream is more powerful and blessed than the richest man on the planet..."

De'Lure

"Once you recognize the fact that NOTHING in your past be it lies or truth, can discount your present accomplishments, or the things you will achieve in the future, life becomes much simpler."

De'Lure

"We are taught to believe that our names and our images are everything... If so that's a good thing because we are in control of all of the above..."

De'Lure

"To read my work… is to peek inside of my very heart and experience my vivid rainbow of imagination"

De'Lure

"When people can't compete with your present, and they fear your future, they have no choice but to bring up and attempt to distort your past"

De'Lure

"We are not who THEY say we are… but exactly who we choose to be"

De'Lure

"If we let the ghosts of our past affect our present and our future… well then we were much better off dying, along with those nagging ghost of long ago…"

De'Lure

"DEDICATION"

I dedicate this book to all of my wonderful friends/readers/investors. I love you all very much, and besides my passion for the art of storytelling you are the main reason I wake up and write every single day. Thank you and I love you all eternally.

"If you're scared of becoming great just attach yourself to somebody who already knows how to fly. You'll never learn how to soar until somebody shows you how to grow your own wings..."

M.L. De'Lure

Personal Investors

Regina Kennedy
Chantay Calhoun
Nneka Henry
Kela King
Twaneshia Powell
Rita Lowry
Charita Leak
Audreka Everett
Valerie Olivier

Syreeta Powell
Katrice Brown
Brandilyn Hayes
Edna Rowell
Cedric Washington
Geri Patterson
Brittney Thrasher
James Bryant
Martenia Shyne
LaShonda Barton-Koonce
George Odom
Jordan Aune
Kriss Mitchell
Tondalaire Ray
Patrick BigRev Milton
Lamar Jones

Welcome all to De'Lure Shorts & Poems 2. The ten new mind-blowingly realistic short stories you'll read in this book will all be later released as either full length novels or Movies. As always my stories are all born from pure imagination, and are written to seem, and feel real but are not to be perceived as such. This is beautiful, gripping, unforgettable fiction... but it is still fiction nonetheless.

Chason Bottom Dollar

(The turbulent life of an 11-year-old millionaire)

God bless Harker Heights, Texas now because I don't think this place has ever been blessed before. My mother Caroline never wanted me, and I don't blame her not even God loves me. I am the definition of the wretched. I am a degenerate that will never amount to anything.

I'm too ugly to even deserve love in any form. My name is Chason Dowden. I'm 11 years old and when the clock strikes 12, I will begin another painful year in my miserable life. I've been with my mother for two years now, ever since she found out my deceased father left me a sizeable trust fund before his passing.

Apparently because of my extreme circumstances, the courts ruled that upon my twelfth birthday my legal guardian could begin receiving $100,000 in my name every 6 months until the trust is empty.

So, two years ago, days after the decision was made, my mother went to a rehab and got herself cleaned up. She got a couple jobs, and everything. She did all of this just so she could regain her custody of me, and wait out the two years until my money begins rolling in. What a mom, right?

She's been quiet all day locked inside her room. This isn't normal for her. She's always at work or in here talking crazy to me or about me. I'm scared. Her venomous words have become a source of comfort to me. At least when she's tearing me down, she's looking at me and talking to me.

Our small two-bedroom apartment is always freezing, and it smells of old vomit and dog pooh. There's never any food in our broken down fridge. It seems like that thing has been leaking forever. I'm wondering, will whatever that smelly liquid is ever run out. The toilet in my mom's room is off limits, and mine has never worked. So I usually wait until I go to school to relieve myself or while she's at work I might sneak outside and use the bathroom behind the dumpster out back.

I usually itch for a while afterwards because I never have any tissue to clean myself. I do take baths, but only once a week. I don't have many clothes to change into anyway so what's the point? My middle school uniform of khakis and a grey shirt is more than just my school uniform. It's the uniform of my life; my pajamas, my play clothes, my court outfit, and even my outfit for church that *one time we went the first Sunday she got me back. I'm about to turn 12 and I feel as though my life is already over.*

The walls are very thin in our measly apartment. I can hear my mother on the phone with her boyfriend Jack.

"I don't want anyone to be able to tell there was any foul play…" he repeats his mother's words.

"She's going to kill me, right now." Chason whispers to himself.

Before his father passed, he gave him a Superman blanket on his 6th birthday. His father told him the blanket was magical and it would always protect him. He told Chason the blanket was more than just a blanket, he said it is his cape and with it he could fly away if he was ever in any danger.

"Damn it, Jack," his mother screams, "I'm gonna do it now I'll call you back when it's done!" She slams the phone down.

"Boy," she yells, "mama needs to talk to you honey…"

Chason quickly rushes to his balcony outside of his bed room window. He looks down to the ground. He knows he's way too high up, to have any chance of a safe landing. His mother burst through the door with a gun in hand.

"Boy what the hell, are you doing?" she asks.

"My name is Chason." he mumbles.

"What did you say to me, boy?" she asks.

"My name is **Chason,** not boy," he shouts, "and I know what you came in here to do."

"I hate you," she tells him, "now come over here and lay down so we can get this over with."

Chason steps on a chair near the balcony and then up onto the balcony itself.

"Boy what the hell, are you doing now?" she exclaims.

"If you come any closer, I'm going to fly right out of this window." he tells her.

"Boy, have you lost your damn mind?" she asks, stepping forward.

"My dad told me this blanket gave me the power to escape danger," he tells her.

"Oh yeah," she says, with a sick smile on her face, "You're just as crazy as he was."

Lifting the gun, she aims it at his head. Chason quickly turns around and jumps off the balcony holding his 'cape' tightly around his neck.

Caroline shoots. The bullet hits him in his upper back. Chason screams out loudly. As his limp body leaves the balcony his 'cape' catches on something causing him to involuntarily swing downward towards the apartment window below his.

His body crashes hard through the thick glass window. Through the blood and glass sticking out of his face he can see a dark figure approaching him. Then everything goes black...

Father may I

Run to your memory

My mother the monster

Is hell bent on killing me

She's the architect of my pain

And the minister of my misery

She says that you were crazy

And that I'm much the same

But she smokes twenty cigarettes a day

And drinks cough syrup from cellophane

You left me a fortune

And that's all she craves

I'd be fine with love and affection

Or at least a soul that could be saved

You gave me my wings

You promised I could fly

The last time I saw you alive

You told me I'd never die

We all die someday

But dad your legacy lives through me

I know you were a kind hearted man

Because your heart beats inside of me

Hopeless Admirer

Carla Tilden has always believed in eternal love and after she got married that belief didn't fade in the least bit. Her single mother taught her at a young age that marriage was about being there until your husband screws up. She taught Carla that no matter what eventually all men cheat and or leave their wives. Carla always doubted her mother's take on men because of the fact that her mother never seemed to be able to keep one.

Carla like most girls began to build her own belief of what men were and ultimately what they would represent in her adult life. Carla became an avid reader at a young age and was mostly into romance novels. As a young adult her favorite author was De'Lure. The first romance novel she ever read was his first romance novel he ever published, "Take My Breath

Away" Orlando Nights. At the time being from Chicago, Illinois, Carla had never been to Orlando, Florida where De'Lure's classic novel was set, but as she read she felt as if she had not only been to the city before, but she felt like it was her home.

She believed with everything in her that the characters in De'Lure's pages were all real people who really went through the things he wrote about. The conversations, emotions, and events seemed all too real to be purely imagination. She believed he changed his character's names so that no one would know who the characters' represent in real life.

Carla's favorite character from "Take My Breath Away" book one through book two was Cameron Jiles. She absolutely fell in love with the woman's strength, and struggles. The love Cameron had for Keldrick Cole, the book's main male character was so real to Carla, and it made her believe she could one day feel that same way about a man as perfectly imperfect as Keldrick Cole.

Carla Tilden is a sweet breathtakingly beautiful dark skinned black woman with short natural hair. Her husband Troy Tilden is exactly what she always dreamed her husband would be. He's handsome, hardworking, and she knows he loves her, but lately his love hasn't felt so obvious. Once you've been privileged to feel like a person's moon, sun, and every star in their sky there is no way to replace that feeling once it's gone.

"Carla..." the voice says from somewhere nearby.

"Carla..." there it is again.

Carla looks up to find her coworker smiling down at her.

"Hey Jason," she blushes, "I'm sorry I was..."

"Daydreaming again right?" he laughs lightly.

"Man," he continues, "I would love to be the cause of all those random thoughts in your mind that always have you so gone."

"Boy," Carla smiles genuinely hitting his hand gently, "I am very married and you are very young…"

"Age ain't nothing but a number Ms. Carla," Jason reminds her, "and I'm twenty-four I'm not a kid."

"Jason," she pats his yellow hand, "I am thirty-six. Believe me I am at a place in my life that your young behind is not ready for. Save yourself."

"Okay Ms. C," he says placing a stack of papers on her desk, "boss said to bring you these."

"What is this Jason?" she asks as he walks away smiling back at her.

"I don't know Ms. C," he teases, "see I'm too young to understand all that."

After work Carla's drive home was too quiet for comfort. She can feel herself falling apart daily piece by piece. After making it into the house she drops all her things near the front door and sits down at her kitchen table.

"Damn it Carla… girl you gotta do better," she whispers to herself, "Troy is falling out of love with me. I know it, I know he is. But what can I do about it?"

Carla stands up from her kitchen table and makes her way to her refrigerator. After opening the door, she stares inside trying to figure out if she should cook dinner or not. Six months ago she would have never given it a second thought, she'd be almost finished cooking by now. Lately her husband Troy hasn't been getting home until after she's already in the bed. He comes in, showers, and goes straight to sleep. Not a kiss, a word, or any form of acknowledgement for his loyal wife. Carla shakes her head and closes the door to the fridge; she doesn't want to waste her time again. She'll just end up eating alone and then putting the leftovers in the fridge to go bad.

The back door opens behind her. Carla turns around.

"Troy…" she wrinkles her brow, "What are you doing here?

"Damn girl," he frowns, "I do live here don't I?"

"Yeah baby," she blushes, "Of course you do. It's just lately…"

"Yeah," he interjects taking his factory jacket off, "what you cook?"

"Well," she swallows, "actually I didn't…"

"Yeah you don't never cook," he growls, "I'll order me a pizza."

"No," Carla laughs uncomfortably, "you don't have to do that love… I can cook…"

"You can cook for me," he interjects, "I can't tell. No its fine I'd rather have pizza than eat you're cooking anyway."

"Babe…" Carla reaches out for him.

"I don't need you to cook for me Carla." Troy tells her.

"But Troy I'm your wife…" she frowns.

"Are you?" he frowns back.

Troy leaves the room without another word and Carla is left to drown in her painful thoughts yet again.

The next day at work Carla can barely keep her eyes open. She spent the night at the kitchen table as she didn't feel welcome in her own room and bed.

"Ms. C…" Jason says standing near her desk.

"Hey Jason," she replies, "You scared me."

"You've been sluggish all day Ms. C are you okay?" he asks.

"Not much sleep last night to be honest." She admits.

"Ah," Jason nods his head twice, "more problems at home huh?"

"Something like that," she smiles noticing how handsome the young man looks in his yellow polo shirt, "and how are you Jason?"

"I'm doing okay Ms. C," he returns her smile, "I'll be a lot better if I can…"

"Jason," she interjects with a nonthreatening hand up, "I told you I am married. Look… you're sweet and if I had met you, years ago I would probably take you up on your offer but…"

"Um Ms. C..." Jason says.

"What Jason?" she replies.

"I was going to say," he smiles, "I'll be better if I can remember the information for my exam this afternoon at the University."

"Oh," she blushes, "I'm so foolish."

"No," he says, "you're gorgeous. And anytime a man speaks to you, you should automatically think he wants to become your everything..."

"I uh..." Carla wrinkles her brow.

"It's true Ms. C." he swears.

"Well thank you Jason." She looks down at her desk no longer capable of staring back into his big brown eyes.

"No, you don't have to thank me Ms. C it's the truth..." Jason insists.

"I have a delivery for a Mrs. Carla Tilden." A tall handsome man says holding a large bouquet of colorful flowers.

"I'm Carla Tilden..." Carla says standing up.

"Then these are for you beautiful," the man hands her the flowers, "whoever sent you these really loves you. I took a glance at the note on the card... you can't fake emotion like that."

"Thank you for bringing these..." Carla smells the flowers deeply.

"Don't thank me," the man smiles at her, "thank whoever the lucky guy is who sent them to you. I gotta run, got more deliveries to make have a wonderful day Mrs. Tilden."

"You too sir..." Carla says as the man walks away.

"Guess home is not so bad after all huh?" Jason sighs.

"I guess not." Carla replies still staring at her flowers.

"That's too bad love..." Jason says unable to take his eyes off the beautiful flowers.

"And why is that Jason?" she asks.

"Well," he sighs, "It's gonna be kinda hard for me to pick up the pieces and become your new man if there are no broken pieces to pick up."

"Oh." Carla smiles at him genuinely.

"Yeah," he tries to smile back, "you look happy though. That's what matters."

"Jason..." Carla says as he walks away and eventually leaves the office all together.

A bouquet of beautiful flowers was delivered to Carla every day for the next two weeks. Every woman in the office is beyond jealous of her now.

"Man you must be doing everything right now Ms. C." Jason says laying a stack of papers on Carla's desk.

"How so," Carla asks, "Mr. Walters is giving me bigger workload every single day..."

"Yeah, I'm not talking about Mr. Walters," Jason explains, "I'm talking about the fact that your husband has been sending you flowers every day for the past thirteen days. And today you received two deliveries."

"Oh," Carla blushes, "it's the strangest thing though Jason... the second bouquet starting coming this week but I have no idea who they could be from... unless my husband..."

"Unless your husband what?" Jason asks.

"It worked," she smiles covering her mouth with her hands, "Oh my God. I can't believe it actually worked."

"Wait," Jason puts a hand on each hip, "what are you talking about? You're not saying you actually believe your husband is... sending you both set of flowers?"

"No," Carla laughs awkwardly, "that would just be unnecessary and redundant Jason."

"I agree," he says cracking a real smile, "which bouquet is more breathtaking to you Ms. C?

"Honestly the second set has been the more satisfying of the bouquets Jason." She admits.

"Wow," he says, "that's..."

"I have to go." Carla stands up from her desk and slides her jacket on and grabs both set of flowers.

"You do," Jason frowns, "we don't get off for three more hours Ms. C."

"I know Jason," Carla pats his shoulder, "I was on this same work schedule when you were still in high school love."

"Right," Jason frowns, "I'm just a kid... I don't understand shit."

"I never said that Jason," Carla frowns, "but I am working hard to save my marriage in a world where most relationships now end in just a matter of months. My husband is on his lunch break I want to go home and surprise him. Is that so terrible?"

"Not at all," Jason picks the stack of papers back up off her desk, "I'll handle these and tell Mr. Walters you had an emergency."

"Jason I..." Carla says.

He walks away and never looks back.

Later that evening at home Carla is asleep on her den sofa. She tried to wait up for Troy but, her tired body had other plans for her.

"Are you serious," his voice booms in the darkness, "what the fuck is this!"

Carla wipes her tired eyes as she sits up on the comfortable blue sofa he never wanted her to buy.

"Cat got your tongue," Troy yells looking down at her, "you've brought home flowers every single day for the past couple weeks and now you have two sets? What the hell is going on Carla?"

"Wait..." she stands up from the sofa.

"No I'm not going to wait," Troy exclaims, "What the hell are you doing woman? You know... it's one thing when a man cheats on his wife. That type of behavior is acceptable and expected. But when a man's wife decides to become a... a whore and step out on him with multiple men... that, that shit is just..."

Carla's eyes are wide.

"You didn't send me these flowers Troy?" she asks.

"Hell no," he laughs harshly, "since when have I ever done some corny shit like that?"

"You used to do things like that all..." Carla says.

"Not in years," he growls, "don't play with me bitch! Who sent you these fucking flowers?"

"I uh," Carla looks down at both beautiful bouquets, "I uh, I honestly don't know hun."

"Oh you don't know," Troy says, "don't worry about it I'm gonna find out."

"Troy..." Carla step towards him.

"What you said before," she swallows, "about men cheating on their wives... are you, were you openly admitting that you cheat on me?"

"This ain't twenty-one questions woman!" he yells.

"I only asked you one." She replies.

"I'm getting outta here you're giving me a damn headache!" Troy grabs his jacket and storms towards the door.

"Troy hunny please... don't leave..." Carla begs.

The door closes behind him. Back on her trusty sofa Carla tries to cry herself back to sleep.

Friday is always the longest day of the week at Carla's job. She didn't want to come in at all today but she knows how badly she needs the hours.

Only one bouquet of flowers came for her today. It came with a card signed the Hopeless Admirer.

"Carla..." a woman says from the other end of the office.

Carla looks around the edge of her cubicle and sees her husband Troy headed her way. She has no time or any place to hide the flowers. Troy is holding a long piece of paper in his left hand.

"You are a joke!" Troy exclaims happily stepping inside his wife's small cubicle.

"Troy what are you doing here," she asks, "and why are you being so loud?"

"Well," he smiles slapping the paper down on her desk in front of her, "this Carla... is a copy of your bank statement. You, desperate lonely bitch, you couldn't name anybody who could possibly be sending your old ass these flowers because you are sending them to yourself!"

The roaring laughter in the office is like sharp daggers piercing every inch of Carla's body.

"And to think," Troy continues, "I was actually jealous for a second... you had me thinking somebody; anybody was interested in being with you..."

"And that would be hard to believe because?" Troy hears the stranger's voice behind him.'

"Who the fuck are you?" Troy asks Jason.

"So you're the luck husband huh," Jason crosses his arms and smiles at Troy, "your wife is everything Mr. Tilden."

"Boy," Troy growls, "I don't know who you are but, you better get your ass outta of here right now!"

"No, I think I'll stay," Jason continues to smile, "Ms. C doesn't look too happy right now."

"She's my wife," Troy steps face to face with Jason, "she's my business not yours."

"Is that so," Jason laughs, "I've never been married before sir but I do know I would never come to my wife's job and publicly embarrass her. What's more *my* wife would never have to send *herself* anything."

"She ain't your wife." Troy growls.

"I'm fine Jason just leave please." Carla cries.

"Yeah punk," Troy pushes him, "leave."

"Don't touch me again sir," Jason says with his smile still intact, "I work here you don't. I'm sure my manager already called the police but I don't need them to handle you. You're way too small for me."

"Fuck you!" Troy exclaims stepping back from the younger but taller man.

"Yeah that's what I thought," Jason laughs, "did you like the flowers today Ms. C? I was gonna do red roses again but I was really feeling the white today."

"What," Carla smiles, "Jason… it was you?"

"It's always been me Ms. C." he admits.

"You're a liar," Troy screams, "She sent those flowers to herself!"

"She sent one set I was sending the other set," Jason clarifies his claim, "I was trying to compete with you, just never imagined you wouldn't be any competition."

"You, son of a bitch," Troy says, "If you touch my wife…"

"I want a divorce Troy…" Carla interjects.

"Sir," one of two police officers says approaching Troy, "you are not under arrest but we are here to escort you out."

"Carla I love you baby," Troy says, "You don't want a divorce I can change baby please…"

"I do and no you can't." Carla stands up as the cop's gentle nudge Troy out of the cubicle.

De'Lure

"So Ms. C," Jason says, "About that first date of ours…"

"Yes Jason I would love to," she says hugging him tightly, "I'm tired but I'm also about to be happily divorced."

Sweet hearts and sour minds

Bitter lies and broken times

The webs we weave

Grow larger by the day

With the power to hide

The things we should say

I love you I need you

I wish you showed me affection

Pay attention to me please

For more than a brief lust session

Or don't get angry when another man

Takes note of my beauty

And feel nothing more than shame

When he takes on the blessing of your duty

I'm your wife you should treasure me

You make me feel like I trapped you

It's obvious I don't have you

And I no longer attract you

I know these are the last days

Of the tragic love we created

But see now I know a man... who knows me well

Finally, I feel appreciated

The hopeFull admirer

Indian Giver

The sun is rising slowly today in the Alabama sky. A soothing breeze is wafting in from the east and an unfamiliar calm has fallen over the city of Montgomery. Wares Ferry Road in east Montgomery is an area that has changed time and time again, due to the fluctuation of new residents over the years. The mentality of much of the youth is to peak now by whatever means necessary and then deal with the consequences when they forcefully present themselves.

My name is Felicia Washington and I find myself feeling sad most times because of the senseless actions of the people around me. There is so much life to be lived; I don't understand why any child or teenager would feel the need to do anything extreme just to make a name for themselves. Why not go to the extreme for some kind of art or academic achievement? Why is every black boy on the planet trying to be a rapper or an athlete?

I'm twenty years old now, but I feel like I'm much older. I read… I read a lot, actually. So much so, that I tend to know more than most of the people I know, or come in contact with. That probably means I hang out with or allow myself to be surrounded by the wrong people far too often.

I've never considered myself the type of weakling that becomes who they are around in an attempt to fit in. But, I notice that the only time I feel the urge to drink, smoke, or listen to certain types of music is when I'm around certain kinds of people. I'm not insecure and I don't feel the need to impress random people or even friends, but sometimes, it's just hard to go against what's popular.

Most people aren't strong enough to make themselves public outcasts; I'm definitely one of those people. It's sad, but he, at least I can admit it. I have five friends that I chill with on a regular basis. None of them are in school and only one of them has a legit job. They don't bring about any immediate danger to my life, but they're damn sure not bettering me either. They're fun, they make me laugh and there is never a dull moment when they're around. They don't care about anything but having fun, which is okay I guess. I mean, we were all still teenagers just a few months ago. But what happens when our bullshit gets old, and we start to have real responsibilities. What happens if my parents get sick or die? What am I going to do?

These are the thoughts that have begun to haunt me lately; I don't want to end up lost in the world without a clue. I don't have any real talent, no dreams; I have no idea who I am or what I'm doing. I mean, people always tell me I'm smart, I should go to college. I'm like okay, and then what? I don't know what I would major in, so I would just be wasting someone's money.

My boyfriend, Charlie, is Native American. He's my escape from everything. We've been dating for about six months now and it feels like we get closer every day. He's the first guy I've ever dated who wasn't black, and I'll admit Charlie is a very refreshing change in the world of dating for me. When we speak I never doubt a thing he tells me, when we arrange something together he's always there on time, and when we're together he really looks at me. It feels so good to be gazed upon and not just gawked at. I have a really nice body, and I understand that attracts a lot of guys. Sometimes though, the reactions and comments are just sickening and disrespectful. With Charlie, it's never like that, he just sees me for me. Even though we've been together for six months, we've never even been close to having sex; we connect on so many other levels. It feels so good to be genuinely liked and cared about. I'm a young black woman who never thought she would date outside of her race, but I must say I'm eternally glad I did. I still love my black men, but I needed something different.

I'm on my way to the mall to meet Charlie now. I haven't seen him in a couple days. It's gonna be nice to taste his full lips again. I try not to let it get to me, but after being in so many relationships where sex was the main component, this thing with Charlie is kind of weird. So, of course I wonder at times if he's even attracted to me in that way. He has to know that if he wanted to make love to me I would let him. He has to know; he has to see that fact clearly in my open eyes. I got my hair done yesterday and I wore this new dress just for him. I hope he likes it.

I'm early, so I'll just wait for Charlie in the food court at our usual meeting spot. He said he would beat me here, but I don't see him so I'll just wait a bit.

"Hey gorgeous," The strong soothing voice says from Felicia's right side.

"Charlie," she smiles standing up to greet him, "where were you?"

"I'm sorry," he hugs her tightly, "I was going to wait, but I had to use the restroom."

"No apology needed, Charlie," Felicia shakes her head, "I'm just glad I get to see you today."

Charlie is wearing tight denim jeans and a black v -neck t-shirt.

"I love your dress," he tells Felicia still admiring her classically beautiful facial features; "it fits you well."

"Thank you baby..." Felicia spins around to give him the full view of her nice green dress.

"And you look perfect, as always," she tells him, "I always liked your long ponytail, but... I don't know. I think I'm digging this. I love the way your hair looks hanging down around your handsome face..."

"I love you." Charlie interjects.

"Yeah, I know," Felicia smiles and then frowns, "wait what did you say?"

"Here, sit down." Charlie says, taking a seat on the bench first.

Felicia sits down next to him, searching his calm eyes deeply.

"Charlie." she says.

"Yes." He replies.

"Did you just say..." she starts.

"I love you, Felicia." He confirms, reaching in his pocket.

"Wait," Felicia holds her hand out to stop Charlie from retrieving the object in his pocket, "what are you doing, Charlie?"

"I have something for you." he says.

"I know it's not a ring, Charlie..." Felicia tilts her head to the side as her brows wrinkle on their own.

Charlie pulls the box out and opens it for her.

"A necklace," Felicia blushes, "Charlie, it's absolutely breathtaking..."

"Turn around so I can put it on you," Charlie says, "There we go. Let me see... It looks perfect on you Felicia."

"Thank you, baby," Felicia leans in to hug and kiss him, "Where did you get this?"

"It belonged to my great-grandmother," Charlie explains, "My great-grandfather gave it to her on their first wedding anniversary. Felicia, this necklace is over eighty years old."

"Why are you..." Felicia starts.

"I already told you," Charlie interjects, "I love you."

"Stop saying that, please," Felecia shakes her head, "you don't love me."

"Okay." Charlie replies.

"Okay," Felicia says, "What do you mean okay? You can't respond to what I said with okay..."

"I told you how I feel," Charlie looks away, "If you don't believe me, I can't force you too."

"Yes you can," Felicia scoots close to him, "that's exactly what you can do Charlie. I like you... I really like

27

you. But it's just weird because you've never even tried to have sex with me..."

"We're not married Felicia." He frowns.

"And this is not the 1920's, Charlie," she smiles, "I don't know, it just makes me feel like you're not attracted to me in that way."

"So, that's what makes you feel attractive to men?" he asks.

"Well, yeah," she admits, "I never..."

"Come on..." He interjects.

Charlie stands up from the bench and heads back in the direction from which he came.

Felicia surveys her surroundings and then quickly follows behind Charlie.

As she follows behind him he passes by every restaurant in the food court and heads into the men's restroom.

Felicia stands there frozen outside the door of the men's restroom.

"What are you doing?" Charlie asks.

"What are you doing," she shakes her head, "I am not coming into the men's bathroom."

"It's Sunday," he reminds her, "we're at Eastdale Mall. Nobody is here but employees."

"So what..." Felicia whines.

28

"You want me to make you feel attractive," Charlie holds his hands out to her, "you think I don't want you in that way let me show you…"

Felicia looks back out towards the food court and no one is in sight. She hesitates a second longer and then takes her boyfriend's hand.

Charlie whisks her into the last stall at the end of the restroom.

"I, I uh…" Felicia stutters.

"Shut up." Charlie says pressing his strong lips against hers.

She smiles looking at his closed eyes.

Charlie reaches in his back pocket as he continues to kiss her.

As his other hands melts from the side of her face Felicia opens her hazel eyes wide. Charlie opens his protection and then unfastens his tight pants. After securing it, he picks Felicia up in the air as she wraps her legs around his waist.

Charlie kisses her deeply as she looks back into his wide eyes.

Felicia can sense his nervousness, so she reaches down and helps guide him to the promised land.

Charlie leans her back against the wall and then gives her all of him.

As soon as it starts it's over.

"I'm sorry…" Charlie's body tenses up and now he can't seem to open his eyes.

After he regains some of his composure, Charlie lets Felicia back down to the floor.

Unable to look her in her eyes Charlie pulls his pants up, fastens them, and then takes a seat on the toilet behind him.

"Charlie…" Felicia whispers.

"Yes." He replies.

"Is this… was that your first time?" she asks.

"Yeah, I'm sorry," he closes his eyes, "I never…"

"Oh no, baby, you don't have to apologize," Felicia says making her way over to him, "this is so sweet. I've never been anybody's… first before."

"So is this how I show you that I love you?" he asks, with a slight scowl on his handsome face.

"I…" Felicia hesitates.

"Because, I don't enjoy sinning Felicia," he growls, "I don't want you to be my black whore, I want you to be my wife."

"Wait," Felicia smiles an evil smile, "Hold the hell up. What did you just say? Because I know damn well you didn't just call me a black whore…"

"How many men have you slept with Felicia?" Charlie asks.

"None of your damn business!" She crosses her arms hard across her chest.

"Okay let's get out of here because you're way too loud…" Charlie says.

"I don't give a damn," Felicia screams, "You just called me a black whore!"

"No," Charlie says, "actually I didn't. I said I don't want you to be that."

"Fuck you, Charlie," Felicia cries, "and you know what, I started to not ever date you in the first place."

"Oh yeah." Charlie stands up.

"Yeah." She replies.

"And why is that?" he folds his arm across his chest as well.

"Because I know my damn history," she tells him, "and I'm not too fond of the lies we're taught in school about the history of your people and mine!

"What the hell does that mean?" he asks.

"Slavery…" she says.

"What does that have to do with me," Charlie exclaims, "I'm one hundred percent Native American, not white!"

"You really don't know do you…" Felicia says stepping back from him.

"Indians owned slaves too, Charlie," Felicia tells him, "black slaves."

"That's just stupid." he replies.

"It's true," she yells, "and don't you ever refer to me as, or mention the idea of me ever being your black whore, you son of a bitch!"

"Fuck you, Felicia," Charlie shakes his head, "Native Americans did not own slaves. You Black people always try to make up bullshit to make the rest of the world feel sorry for you."

"Native American owned slaves, Charlie," she yells, "and they didn't do it to try to seem civilized to impress the white people who were stealing their land away. The Indians were fully aware of what they were doing and openly bought and sold black slaves."

"Prove it." Charlie shrugs his shoulders.

"You arrogant little bastard," Felicia says, "Google, Barbara Krauthammer. She wrote a book called "Black Slaves, Indian Masters". It's true, but most people like you have no idea."

"Give me my necklace back." Charlie says.

"Five tribes were known to own black slaves…" Felicia says.

"Give me my necklace back…" He repeats.

"The Cherokee, Creek, Chickasaw, Choctaw, and the Seminole's all owned black slaves." Felicia tells him.

"This is why we don't date black girls!" Charlie snatches the necklace from around Felicia's neck and storms out of the stall.

Felicia follows closely behind him.

"Damn," Felicia says, "you sure fall out of love quick, huh…"

Charlie turns to face her.

Why should I run from my future

When I never can hide from my afflictions

I'm frowned upon by circles of my peers

Because I enunciate and speak with perfect diction

They hate me so but I'm no better than them

I have no clue what I want to be

But I refuse to die in the city I was born in

There's a whole world I'm waiting to see

I have a man

But I don't know if he's still mine

We usually get along great

As long as I don't speak my mind

It's easy to be proud of your heritage

Especially if you don't know the whole truth

I know what I know and I studied my origin

So I cling firmly to my roots

I can educate anyone

If they're willing to learn

I don't say this in arrogance

I too have knowledge to earn

But I listen and I respect truth

Logic is not a foul word

My powerful thoughts keep me above stagnation

Like the wings of a clever bird

Life after Love

"It'll be a cold day in hell when me and her get back together bro," Carlton claims, "That bitch is crazy."

Carlton's friend Jonathan laughs, but he knows his friend's words to be a fact.

"Who's crazy?" Veronica asks, walking into Carlton's bedroom.

"What are you doing here," Carlton groans, "and why are you in my room?"

"Well, I'm here because you're the father of my children," Veronica claims, "and I'm in **your room** and not **your house** because your grown ass still lives **here** at **ya mama's house**."

"What do you want, fam?" Carlton pauses his videogame and sits up on his bed.

"Carlton, do not call me fam," Veronica places a firm hand on her left hip, "I am not fam. I'm bae, baby, baby mama…"

"Yeah, you my baby mama, that's about it." Carlton says.

"My patna don't want you no more, Veronica," Jonathan tells her, "but you do look good in them tight ass pants though."

"Shut up, Jonathan," Veronica snaps, "this fool only fronting because you here."

"I don't gotta front for nobody," Carlton says, standing up face to face with Veronica. "You need to leave, fam."

"Stop talking to me like I'm a dude," Veronica pushes Carlton back down, "and stop acting like you don't love me…"

"I'm not actin'." Carlton says.

Jonathan bursts into laughter at the look on Veronica's confused face.

"Come outside, Carlton." Veronica says.

"For what?" he asks.

"Just put on some shoes and bring yo ass outside," Veronica demands, and then storms out of his room.

As she stands outside his mother's front door, Veronica can't help but to pace back and forth.

Finally, Carlton emerges from the front door.

"Really, Carlton…" Veronica says.

"Why you gotta play me in front of my friend though, bae?" Carlton asks.

"Boy, you are twenty-four years old," Veronica screams, "grow the fuck up, please! Why are you doing this childish ass shit?"

"Doin what?" Carlton asks. "And, I am grown."

"No you are not, Carlton," Veronica pushes him, "now you got a decent job and you help me with our kids, but you still dealing with yo same dumbass homeboys. Why can't you just let em go?"

"For what?" Carlton asks.

"What you mean?" Veronica replies.

"Let my homies go, for what," he asks, "why would I do that? They're not causing me no harm."

"They're not helping you grow either, Carlton, damn!" Veronica turns her back on him.

"Look," Carlton says, "you know I love you, and I love my kids…"

"See." Veronica says.

"See what," Carlton replies, "and why you cut me off while I was talking?"

"This is the shit I'm talking about, Carlton," she says, "you just sat in there and told that fool you don't love me. You have more loyalty to those fools than you **ever** had to me."

"Oh, let's not talk about loyalty…" Carlton laughs.

"Oh, shut the hell up, Carlton!" she growls.

"You cheated on me with a chick, remember." He says.

Veronica stares a venomous hole through him.

"Oh, now you mad?" he smiles, stepping close to her.

"Don't smile at me," she says, stepping back, "and do not touch me."

"This is childish," Carlton says, "I might as well take my ass back in the house."

"Yeah, you might as well." Veronica agrees with crossed arms.

Carlton turns to leave.

"If you touch that door knob, Carlton Andrew Miles, I swear to God I will burn this mother fucka' down!" Veronica warns him.

"This is why all my friends say you're crazy." Carlton steps back from the door.

Veronica doesn't reply.

"You can't say shit like that," Carlton tells her, "you sound like you mean that shit, and when my boys hear that typa shit…"

"I don't care," she screams, "don't you understand those assholes are the reason we broke up. You spent all your time with them or running behind bitches with them and you broke my heart a million times."

"Nah, I don't think it was a million times," Carlton smiles.

"It's not funny, Carlton." Veronica wipes her face.

"Wait, are you crying?" Carlton steps forward and wraps his arms around her.

"Nah," she says, "you're not worth crying over anymore."

"Then why the hell are you crying, Veronica?" he asks.

"Because…" she says.

"Because what, fam?" Carlton asks.

"I am standing here, trying with everything I am to love you again," she admits, "and I can't. I really have no words for you, Carlton."

"Like that, huh?" Carlton says, backing away.

"Yeah," she cries, "it's exactly like that, exactly like you made it."

"So why the hell you even over here, fam?" he asks.

"I came to let you know…" she looks down at her feet.

"You came to let me know what?" Carlton walks up close to his ex again.

"I, uh," she hesitates, "I kinda met someone."

Carlton laughs.

"I'm serious, Carlton." Veronica doesn't blink once as she stares back at him.

"Oh, you... you're serious right now?" he asks.

Veronica wipes more tears away.

"So that's how we doing it now?" he continues.

Veronica takes a few steps back.

"Say something, V," Carlton says, "I mean, damn for six years, it's always just been me and you... now you went and..."

"Just me and you," Veronica laughs through new tears, "is that some kind of fucking joke, Carlton?"

"Hell no." he replies.

"Well, it's a damn lie," Veronica screams, stepping forward to push him as hard as she can. "You've had sex with my friends, my cousin, and you tried my sister a couple of summers ago! Yeah don't look surprised now, dude. She been told me, but she didn't want to start any shit and then be the reason we broke up. So, my dumbass just ate that shit and never said a word. Do you have any idea how embarrassing that shit is when bitches come tell me you had sex with them or tried them? And you have the nerve to bring up me being with a girl one time... and I did it for you..."

"Man, I wasn't there, so it wasn't for me," Carlton says, "and I can't help that all your people wanna get at me because I look good, bae... They're just jealous of us..."

"Yes, Carlton," she starts, "you are the most attractive guy I have ever dated we both know that. But, you have never been faithful to me. We are grown now, Carlton, we have two kids... and no plan for a future as a family."

"Yes, we do…" Carlton tries to get close enough to hold her.

"All those girls, Carlton," Veronica shakes her head as she holds him away from her, "All those damn girls. Do you feel like a **man,** huh… do you feel **accomplished**? Was it worth breaking my heart **over and fucking over, again**?"

"But bae, I never **dated** them," Carlton says, "it was just sex…"

"God damn it, Carlton!" Veronica lunges forward, tackling Carlton hard to the ground.

"**It… doesn't… matter… you… dumb… ass!**" With every word, Veronica hits the father of her children with all her might.

"**Why, why, why**," Veronica cries, climbing off of Carlton, "Why am I here, why am I fighting with you… its childish and I'm tired Carlton."

"The truth is," Veronica continues, "I'm not just seeing this guy… We've been dating for a while… and he's asked me and the kids to move in with him."

"No." Carlton dusts himself off as he stands back to his bare feet.

"I told him, yes," Veronica admits, "this man… **my man** wants something with me **and my children** that you're just not capable of giving us."

Veronica turns to leave.

Carlton reaches deep in his pant pocket for the thing he's been carrying around every single day for the past two months just trying to find the right time to reveal it.

De'Lure

"Bae..." Carlton says, as she continues to walk towards her car.

"What Carlton..." as Veronica turns around she sees her first love finally down on one knee and holding out to her the prettiest ring she's ever seen in her life.

In love... a bad perception can become reality

If we fight how we truly feel

And once we come to our senses

Often times the wounds are too old to heal

How can a man turn his back on love

To remain relevant to his past

A good wife is a wonderful thing

And great wonders are meant to last

Fear of change and the threat of commitment

Are thoughts that can be broken

Never force a boy to be a man

His mind and heart must first be open

Once he has changed give him a chance

Don't let the past block out your delight

True love can be a cure and a perfect map

To riveting reoccurring romantic nights

Love Down

"*I love how the moon awakens the night, as its friendly stars adorn the sky ever so peacefully. I've always believed that the world is just a little more beautiful from my old backyard. My name is Stephanie Miller; I'm thirty-seven years old and well past my prime. I know, I know they say you are only as old as you so feel. I haven't had the hardest life but this old body feels all thirty-seven of these years it has endured. Haaa ha ha ha. Now, that laugh felt so good. You know, married women shouldn't sit alone most nights in their backyards staring up into the skies pondering all the things that could have been. Not a married woman and especially not a married woman who's nearing her fifteenth wedding anniversary. Ahhh… when the wind blows, so does my hair, yielding to its power. You wouldn't think my thick*

natural curls would get as much movement as they do, due to the flow of the wind but they move and flow, baby. Lord... hmm, I remember when my man... my husband used to adore me. It seems so long ago now. How much time has run away, and how much have I changed that those sincere sentiments that man once felt for me could be that much of an afterthought? Am I that disgusting, am I far too old now... have I become unforgivably undesirable? If I have..., if I am now only a shred of what that man... my man once was so in love with, I duly apologize. It's my fault. Once that man made me his wife, and committed his life and future to me, it became my job to keep myself together so that his eyes... and other things wouldn't one day begin to wander..."

"Steph," a voice says from nearby, "What you doin out here girl... you out here talking to ya self again, love?"

"How much did you hear Jen?" Stephanie asks.

"Enough girl," Jen replies, "more than enough."

Stephanie shakes her head gently staring down in her lap.

"Steph..." Jen starts.

"Yeah girl..." she replies.

"Can you... will you, pray with me honey?" Jen asks, with her concerned brows wrinkled tightly.

"I thought you'd never ask, girl..." Stephanie smiles as a new tear streams down her aging, round, black face.

Jennifer Larkin, the younger of the two women, leans forward and wipes her friend's lone tear away just before it reaches her chin, and then takes both of her cold hands in her own.

"Had to stop that tear from touching the ground..." Jen tells Steph.

"Oh yeah," Stephanie sniffs, trying to hold back more tears from peeking through, "why is that?"

"If a tear doesn't touch the ground," Jen smiles, "you can take it back. That tear never existed, and I'm glad it didn't."

"What are you talking about, Jennifer?" Steph asks.

"Michael does not deserve your tears girl," Jen tells her, "he never did. I want you to never cry for his sorry ass ever again. I wish we could together un-cry every tear you ever blessed him with."

"Now, I know I'm old," Steph laughs a bit, "but honey, please tell me how you bless someone with tears?"

"Every tear you've ever cried for that man was a public symbol of your love and affection for him," Jen explains, "and he doesn't deserve that power... **not anymore**."

"Wait a minute," Steph pulls her hands away from her younger friend and neighbor, "Jen do you... know something you're not telling me? Are you sleeping with my husband?"

"**First** of all," Jen says, "Your husband is fifty, and I'm not interested in a sugar daddy. Second of all, my husband is gorgeous **and young**. And lastly I thought we were friends Mrs. Miller..."

"So now I'm Mrs. Miller," Stephanie smiles at Jennifer, "now I feel old all over again."

"Well when you start saying things like what you just said I can't help but to believe you just might be getting a little senile."

"Watch ya mouth girly..." Steph says as they share a laugh.

"Just kidding girl..." Jen assures her.

"Now what happened to that prayer you promised me Jennifer?" Steph asks.

Jen takes Stephanie's hands in hers again.

"Lord God," Jen begins, "Heavenly father up above... my Creator... The Alpha and the Omega... please give Mrs. Miller the strength to leave her old wrinkly, mean, unfaithful ass husband. Lord I..."

"Jennifer what the hell is this..." Stephanie laughs pulling her hands back once again.

"Girl," Steph continues, "you ain't never done much praying, have you girl?"

"Not really... but I meant every word." Jen confirms confidently.

"Well darling', you started off fine," Steph tells her angry friend, "but I think maybe you got lost in the moment... but name calling and swear words aren't usually part of holy prayers."

"Wait a minute now," Jen says, "Now what's the difference between a holy prayer and my prayer?"

"Jennifer, I appreciate everything you do for me I really do," Steph says, "and your relationship with God is between you and Him. I would just personally prefer not to be a part of a prayer that... girl what am I talking about? Here I go, just ramblin' on..."

"No Mrs. Miller," Jen says, "you're right. I'm not a praying woman and since I don't know how, I needed to be corrected."

"Its fine, honey..." Steph gently rubs her knee closest to her.

"It's not," Jennifer exclaims, "I'm sorry Mrs. Miller... but I have so much respect for you and how you hold on to Mr. Miller, but he don't deserve it. He don't deserve it all Mrs. Miller."

"Jennifer, are you crying?" Steph leans close to her friend.

"Well, I ain't sad if I am," Jen wipes her face roughly as Steph slides over and wraps her arms around her, "I'm not sad Mrs. Miller, I'm mad as hell. I wish you would just leave his sorry ass."

"Jennifer," Steph says, "I never told you this... but when Mike and I first got married, I knew I couldn't have children, but I never told him. I was afraid he would break the engagement off, and being married at the time just seemed like the answer to all of my problems as a twenty-two-year-old woman. I was feeling like if somebody didn't marry me soon that meant something had to be wrong with me... you know? And I just, I couldn't bare losing Mike... So, I kept it a secret."

"Oh my God," Jen gasps with both hands over her mouth, "and what happened when he..."

47

"When he found out," Steph interjects with an uncomfortable laugh, "let's just say once my husband found out I couldn't bear children... he decided he not only could have children with other women but he could cheat on me whenever he pleased."

"So why did you stay, Mrs. Miller?" Jen asks.

"That's what women do child," Steph smiles, "we stay..."

"Like hell." Jen replies.

"What you say?" Steph wrinkles her forehead.

"No hell we don't stay," Jen reiterates as she stands up from the almost comfortable backyard bench, "Hell no, not when we are being used, abused, disrespected... Mrs. Miller, and I'm sorry to keep calling you that, but I'm having a hard time not talking to you like you're my age because of the things you're saying, so I have to keep reminding myself that you are my elder. I don't mean any disrespect to you, but you are living a foolish life."

"No, I agree Jennifer," Stephanie admits, "please sit back down."

Jennifer obeys.

"What would you have an old woman like me do?" Steph asks her young neighbor.

"Girl," Jen rolls her slim neck, "you better run away somewhere like Stella and get yo damn **groove** back."

"I'm too old for all that child..." Steph laughs awkwardly.

"Not funny, and what does that even mean," Jen asks, "You're not that old Mrs. Miller."

"I'm too old to run away," Steph claims, "I don't work, I haven't worked in years, and all my money is Mike's money."

"Exactly," Jen says, "that fool did not make you sign a prenup, so his money damn sure is your money. And you can work; you just haven't in a little while."

"Try eight years." Steph says.

"You can work." Jen tells her.

"I don't want to be alone though Jennifer." Steph admits.

"Girl," Jen replies, "you got a whole live in husband and you are lonely as hell."

"I can't argue with that." Steph wipes new tears away.

"Hey," Jen says, "You know I don't read much but it's something about that man De'Lure."

"Who?" Steph asks.

"He's an author," Jen explains, "yesterday I was reading a funny but very interesting article he wrote in his magazine titled "Love Down". In the article he explained that men and women of all races can find maybe not love, but supreme loyalty and comfort by seeking companionship with someone we may have never considered dating seriously before. Relax your standards a bit Mrs. Miller."

"So, you're telling me to date a bum?" Steph asks.

"No," Jen smiles, "just date down love…"

"Date a bum?" Steph says again.

"Find a… slightly broken man," Jen says, "and fix him."

"Leave my husband of fifteen years," Steph says, "and begin dating a bum."

"Look," Jen replies, "Mike's old ass has it all. You've been with him all this time and you ain't happy. So try something new, since obviously money, cars, and clothes haven't made you happy. You could *probly* find a homeless man on the side of the street who could treat you a lot better than that asshole."

"There's my gorgeous wife." The raspy voice says, entering the backyard.

Jen feels her entire body growing tense.

"Hey, babe," Steph smiles, over her shoulder, at her husband.

"Hello Jennifer." Mike says, as he kisses his wife on top of her natural head.

"I was just leaving," Jen says, brushing past him, "good night."

Jennifer rushes back to her own empty house. As she lies there staring at the candle light, she finds herself lost in her own empty thoughts again. Pain is such a powerful nuisance and escape for the bewildered.

Meanwhile Michael and Stephanie are still in their backyard.

"Come inside, we need to talk." Mike says with a strange tone.

"Okay," Steph says, still seated on her padded backyard bench, "but, I..."

"Now," He says with finality, as he makes his way inside the house.

Steph carefully blows out the blue and white scented candles on the windowsill behind her star gazing bench and meekly heads towards the uncomfortable living space that she calls home. As she rounds the corner inside her back door, she stops cold as everything inside of her begins to crumble.

"Wait," Steph mumbles, "what is this, what's going on Michael...?"

"Wait, wait," her husband mocks her harshly, "What is this Michael... It is time for you to leave Stephanie."

"Are you crazy?" the tears have returned to their rightful home, plaguing Stephanie's round black face two at a time.

"Yes actually, I am," Michael replies, "I have been insane for fifteen years. See, I continued to live this lie with you, day in and day out, just hoping that one day I'd come home from work and find you gone... or better yet, just dead. I would then call the police and make a report about your inevitable suicide..."

"Suicide," Steph cries. "Mike, why would I commit..."

"Why would you not, is the question," Mike interjects, "I have been nothing short of deteriorating to you. I have gone out of my way to make sure no joy for you lived inside these walls. I didn't want to hear your parents' mouths, but see, they're both dead now."

Mike and his companion laugh harshly.

"Those old black bastards finally kicked the bucket," he continues, "hallelujah saints, Amen! So, now that your parents are deceased I need you to be deceased to me."

"Mike, who is she?" Steph points at the young white woman sitting at her kitchen table. "And why is she in our house."

"You still don't get it, huh?" he steps closer to his lover and bends down to kiss her full on the lips.

The shred of sanity left inside of Stephanie Miller passed away the moment her husband's lips touched that of his whore in front of her broken face.

"We," Mike begins, "have separate bank accounts now..."

"No we don't," Steph cries, "we do not have separate accounts, I just used my debit card on our joint account yesterday to buy candles and flowers... and..."

"I had it done today," Mike says, "you can keep the truck and you have enough money to stay in a hotel until you find a small apartment somewhere."

Michael hands his wife her keys to her vehicle.

"Go now," he says, "Don't make this harder than it has to be, Steph..."

"Don't you ever speak my name again," she cries, "never! This is what you chose over a woman who lived and died for you every single day for fifteen years! You chose this, this slut over me! This is what you want?"

"Just leave, Mrs. Miller," the woman says, "you don't know me…"

"Bitch," Stephanie screams, "you do not…. Are you fucking kidding me? Did you just address me?"

"I'm just saying," the woman continues, "we don't know each other, so…"

Stephanie rushes towards the woman, Mike quickly steps in the way. With strength not even she knew she had, she knocks her husband down to the floor as his new woman tries to scamper away. Stephanie reaches out instinctively and grabs the woman by her long blonde ponytail and snatches her down to the ground.

With the woman's neck clutched tightly in her hands, Mrs. Miller forgets her husband is even in the room, as she says, "You are right, I do not know you, but you knew about me and you still chose to sleep with my husband. For that… bitch, you deserve the hell that will be your future with him."

"Okay…" the much smaller woman squeezes the word out through her closed throat.

"I could kill you now…" Steph says.

Whap!!!

Mike slaps his wife across the back of her head sending her flying towards the back door.

53

"Leave, bitch," Mike demands.

"I'm your wife, Michael!" she screams.

"Some wife," he scoffs, helping his new woman to her feet, "Stephanie, your dusty ass eggs couldn't even give me a child."

"I can't have children because I got raped brutally when I was just twelve years old Mike," she screams through her tears, "and you know that!"

"Well whoever raped you," Mike says, "if they could see you now, they'd all spare you this time."

"Noooo!" Steph rushes towards her evil husband.

He quickly pulls out a gun from a holster on the back of his belt.

Sitting in my backyard alone

Head back eyes lost in the stars

Dreaming of a new hope

To placate my pain and hide my scars

You'll know no greater pain than knowing

Your love is no longer yours

Not even if you pierce your skin with knives

And pour salt in your gaping sores

He could have another life without me

But why couldn't he leave me first

How can I ever let go

Of the man who gave my soul birth

Home late every night

See the streets are more attractive

The love of a good wife at home

Could never be as vital or impactive

As cheap whores

Or rounds of beer with the guys

Surely all the love is gone

When he no longer feels the need to lie

I don't love you anymore

Damn it... I don't even think I want to

Those were the words my husband said to me

He snatched my heart and my soul is gone too...

A Preacher's Admission

Father, I can no longer run from the things that I see and feel. As I speak to my congregation... often times I feel myself almost shaming them into cheering me on, singing along with my deceitful voices, and financing this church. I say "voices" Lord, because I feel as if at times Satan himself is working and speaking through me. I am so ashamed of what I have allowed myself to become. As I now grow older, I no longer know what is fact or what is fiction. A white man once told me that God and the Bible were not created for my people. I am a black man, God, as You know, and honestly on the one hand I have to be inclined to agree with what that white man told me that day. My ancestors were enslaved for hundreds of years and told that the

Bible upheld and vindicated the white man's right to own them. Why Lord, why Jesus... Why are there so many questions circling throughout my mind? Why do I feel now when I pray to You my words and my agenda are not sincere? Have You left me Lord...? I know full well the Word says You will never, ever leave me or forsake me, but at times I feel more than forsaken. I am the leader of a church, and in my mind I know that I am now more lost than an ignorant infant suckling his mother's breast on the back row of my sanctuary. Lord, I am losing this church. They know... the people can see. The money that is being pumped into this church is no longer being used as it should. It pays my rent; it pays my car note. It has financed unsavory trips that I've taken with random women in the church. Those whores are all in love with me. They worship the ground I walk on. I can, and almost have slept with every man's wife in my congregation. They come see me late at night here at the church for "private counseling sessions" and they proceed to do anything I instruct them to do. After I finish with them, they ask me to pray over them. It's sick. The missionary position contrary to what many of them believe is obviously not actually an act of God. These women... the women of my church are so lost, and more than blind to who and what I am. They're so ignorant it's almost as if they believe that by having sex with me, and succumbing to my every desire, they can somehow sleep their way into Heaven. And I am no better than them because I allow them to believe such utter foolishness. You already know all these things, my God. I hope You punish me well... But, in turn, give my flock a pass. Forgive those whores and simpletons, as they obey and finance me, they know not what they do. They believe in me, but I believe in You, oh God. I have never actually seen a miracle with my own eyes. But, I continue to tell my church, every Sunday, to expect your own miracle today! They never see those miracles, but the possibility that they might experience a miracle one day keeps them coming back, week after week. I yell when I preach because I feel as though the louder I speak to them, the more believable my words become. I told them today, that You will restore the years that the "locusts" have eaten. I believed my damn self when I lied to them today. But Lord, how can I preach that You will restore lost years to them, when all my dead years You allowed me to lose have yet to be restored to me? I'm angry, bitter, and poor, Lord God. I know full well this is the final year I will have this church. I have survived this long because of the intellect You blessed me with. Every successful pastor must be the most intelligent man in his church. This is nothing more than a game that I'm playing with my congregation week in and week out... I portray a wondrous character that I play every time I enter into that pulpit. None of it is real. Do not forgive me Lord, forgive my flock... And in the end, as You rightfully send me to burn eternally down below, allow my ignorant sheep to ascend into your Heavenly Gates.

Heavenly Father

Please... rain down instructions for your son

I am lost and fading fast

In the midst of a battle the devil has won

I used my gift

To fool people and finance my life

I pretend to love them

And understand their pain and strife

I'm the wolf in sheep's clothing

I'm even a danger to myself

You blessed me with a gorgeous wife

Lilian still loves me to death

I don't deserve her company

Or her love and faith

I wonder what her life could have been

If she denied me... her cringe worthy fate

I've lead them all astray

My wife, my kids, and my flock

I've failed miserably at showing them truth

But in the end You are still my rock

Stroganoff

The year is 2032. You would think by now maybe we'd have flying cars and maybe even hovering houses. We don't, things have changed… but not quite for the better, at least not for most people. The world is strange now and more than cold. The streets are filled with angry youths with no focus or purpose. In 2032 here in America, either you're very rich or you're not. Everybody in this neighborhood is not.

In some respects, the world is much better now. The food is exceptional. The Illuminati was exposed and dethroned about five years ago, and every aspect of the American government they secretly controlled, was wiped clean and restarted. So now, none of the chemicals that had been put in American food that was slowly killing people for the past few centuries exist anymore.

You can now eat forever off one food supply, if you can afford it. For $10,000,000 you can buy a lunch case. Whatever food you put inside your lunch case will continue to replenish itself forever. You can always add new food items inside a lunch case. Once an item is added to a case's menu by pressing a few buttons on the case's keypad, you can enjoy any dish on the menu at any time in minutes. No one in this neighborhood would know anything about lunch cases.

Every ghetto looks pretty much the same in the new world. The Amberella Stone projects are among the worst though. Buck Songers, a poor aging black man has lived on Broadway Street in the Amberella Stone projects for the past ten years. The neighborhood is more than dangerous but nobody ever bothers him.

Standing out on his front porch, looking in the distance, Buck knows everything about his meaningless life is about to change forever.

From the end of the street comes a long fancy red limousine. The young people standing in the street part like the red sea as the car passes between them like a great royal carriage.

The Limo itself seems to emit rays of protection and dominance, so much so that the young street thugs in the vicinity of it don't even consider trying to rob whoever's inside.

"Mother," London says.

"Yes dear?" her mother replies.

"What time are you and papa gonna pick me up from school today," she asks, "I want to go out to eat after school mother."

A tall, fat Black man approaches the car.

"How do…" he says, in mock adoration to the ritzy family.

"You must be Buck?" the girl's father says.

"I am…" the man replies.

"Fine," the father nods his stiff head, "Here are her bags. There's never ending beef stroganoff in her lunch case among other treats she loves to eat. Take everything inside, and after we run up the street to the bank, we're going to bring her right back."

"Yes sir." Buck says flashing an awkward smile down at the pretty little white girl. Buck obediently takes the bags and the case inside, as the red limo makes its way down Broadway Street to the bank.

Minutes later Buck looks out of his front window, to see the red limo return. It parks again in the very same spot. On the front steps of Buck's house is a white teenage boy named Parson. Parson is also watching the strange family inside the fancy red limo.

He's jealous because he never had parents, but at the same time he feels drawn to this family and the little girl. Parson hates everything and everybody, but for some reason he doesn't hate them at all, but he is wondering why they're here.

A strong breeze wafts in from the side of him. Parson pushes his long blonde hair back out of his calm hazel eyes.

As the little girl inside the limo continues to talk looking down at her writing pad with a red pen in hand, both of her parents kiss her gently on the forehead before stepping out of the car. Then the two of them quickly jump into another car that pulls up next to the limo and they speed off.

As Buck approaches the limo, he notices the girl is still talking to her absentee parents and writing on her little pad.

"You can get out of the car now, princess…" Buck says with a toothy grin.

"Is it time for class to start already," London replies, "Where did you put my backpack? All my prescriptions for my new classmates are in there."

All the kids at London's old school pretended to love when she diagnoses them with made up illnesses, and then gives them her imaginary prescriptions from her red backpack.

"You won't be needing your backpack, little girl," Buck says laughing to himself, "This ain't no school, darlin'."

"Wait," London says, "What do you mean this isn't a school? Then what is it, and where did my parents go?"

"I'll be right back. I need to go get the paperwork."
Buck says laughing to himself, as he reenters his house.

The warm tears rush London's face before she can
stop them. She wants to be strong, but for the first time in
her life nothing around her makes any sense, and her vivid
imagination isn't vivid enough to hide her from her new
developing harsh reality.

Parson feels his heart beating in his heart chest as
he watches the little girl cry all alone in the long car. He
jumps up and rushes inside the house. Minutes later,
Parson emerges with a gorgeous hybrid flower in hand. He
rushes to the side of the limo London is sitting on and
opens the door.

"Hey, can I sit with you…" he asks handing her the
beautiful flower.

London shrugs her shoulders, as she scoots over
to allow him to get in.

"I'm Parson," he tells her, "What's your name?"

"London," she cries, "I'm not supposed to be here…
wherever here is."

"Yeah, that much I can tell." he says, looking down
at her expensive designer shoes.

"Now isn't that sweet," Buck says, through the car
window on the opposite side from them, "Both of my new
orphans making nice together already."

"Shut the hell up, Buck!" Parson demands.

"Orphan," London says, "I ain't no orphan, I mean
I'm not an orphan. My parents just…"

"Left," Buck says, "Your parents left you here with me little girl. I can't say too much, and you ain't gonna make me either. They paid me a sizeable amount to take care of you until you come of age… and such duties is what I'm here for. So if you would just sign here on the dotted line…"

"I don't even know you!" London says, staring a hole through Buck's big yellow teeth and eyes.

"Allow me to introduce myself," Buck says, with another toothy grin, "I'm Buck Songers and you now live with me in my wonderful group home."

London looks up at Parson for the first time. She notices his hazel eyes are almost as pretty as hers. She smiles at the comfort in them, even though she's anything but comfortable now.

"Just sign," Parson tells her, returning her strange smile, "Trust me, it could be much worse. The group home I just left was like a prison. We couldn't even go outside. Buck's an asshole, but at least he seems to be a lenient asshole."

London reluctantly signs the form with her own pen. Then, Parson opens the door and escorts her inside. As soon as they step inside the house, the foul smells begin to assault London's privileged nose.

"Wow," she says, "what is that smell?"

"Home…" Parson sighs solemnly.

"You'll get used to it," he continues, "Every group home in New York smells like this… or at least I think they do."

London is paying close attention to everything, and the filth that surrounds her is almost too much for her ten-year-old stomach.

As they pass through the kitchen, London grabs her expensive lunch case.

"You hungry..." London says smiling awkwardly up at Parson.

"Always..." he replies, with a handsome smile of his own.

Later that afternoon Parson and London are sitting on the front porch observing some neighbors. Two black teen girls are arguing right in front of Mr. Songers' house.

"Whatever you kids do," Buck says from the doorway, "Don't leave this yard without my permission. It's not safe."

"Yeah, whatever," Parson replies without looking back, "I guess I lied London, this place is like a prison too.

Buck stands firm in the doorway now with a hand on each aging hip.

London shakes her curly blonde head.

"So what's going on with your parents?" Parson asks London.

"I don't know," London replies, "But I'm done crying, I'm sure this is all just a mistake. They'll be back to pick me up later. My parents can't survive without me Parson."

"Yeah I hope you're right kid," he replies, "cause, you ain't built for this life."

"Parson," Buck says, "Sorry to interrupt again, but do not walk your white ass off these premises without my permission or else..."

Parson and London both ignore the eavesdropping Buck and focus back in on the two black girls, arguing over some boy at the edge of the yard.

One girl has on the brightest yellow sweater London has ever seen in her life. In the center of it is a huge protruding live sunflower. The other girl's shirt has red roses growing out of the center of it, that are all swirling up around her head in a strangely intriguing fashion statement.

Both of them are wearing leggings that are changing color by the second. As the two of them head down to the end of the street in obvious rage, Parson begins to follows them.

"Parson you heard what Buck said, it's not safe to leave the yard..." London reminds him.

Once they reach the other end of the street, they begin fighting each other fiercely. Parson takes a seat on a nearby car and watches the fight with a real smile on his face. He glances back in the direction of the house to assess just how far he actually walked to see the fight.

"It's not that far..." he mumbles to himself as he refocuses on the two angry girls. Parson hopes the two girls slaughter each other.

The girl with sunflower on her sweater is absolutely destroying the girl with the roses all around her head. Parson can tell the rose wearer is a much better fighter, but her stupid shirt is blocking her vision so the smaller girl is getting the best of her.

After the fight is over, Parson walks back up the block to the group home. He notices the black street thugs looking at him strangely. Some of them are even licking their lips as if they plan to eat him or something.

"What's the word, fool..." a tall skinny black boy says, as Parson passes by him.

Parson ignores him and keeps walking straight. By his calculation he's about two hundred feet away from Songer's house.

Another black teen approaches him, swinging his hand really low as if he wants Parson to shake hands with him. Parson does. As soon as Parson touches the stocky light skinned teen's hand, he realizes it was a mistake.

Everything around Parson has grown completely silent, and all eyes are on him. The flowers on all the girl's shirts are still now and nobody's clothes are changing colors anymore. Parson doesn't break a sweat as he turns to look at the big kid whose hand he hit.

"What the hell was that, fool?" the boy asks Parson.

"I thought you were... Never mind man." Parson says, as he starts back walking.

As he takes his third step he can feel the boy's hand coming at him fast. Parson ducks and then punches the boy twice in the face knocking him out cold. Two more boys rush Parson and they get the same treatment.

Parson can see more and more young guys readying themselves to attack him.

"Parson!" Mr. Songers yells, from the porch of his raggedy old house.

Parson hesitates as more thugs approach him and then breaks out in a sudden dead sprint to the house. He's almost there but the boys behind him are getting closer.

As he makes it to the house, all of his pursuers run into some kind of invisible force field surrounding Songers' yard. Parson looks back at the bullies staring through the invisible wall at them in awe.

"Parson, get your ass in this house now," Buck yells, "And you too, little miss sunshine!"

Upstairs in their room, Songers sits both kids on the bed and closes the door behind him. He reaches inside each one of their shirts and pulls out identical necklaces.

Parson and London look at each other with wrinkled brows.

"Weird." they say, in unison.

"Not really," Buck says, "Don't the two of you geniuses find it strange that this is a group home and you two are the only two kids in it?"

"I just figured some of the other kids outside lived here too…" Parson says standing up from the bed.

"Sit down, boy." Buck growls.

"Hell no, Buck," Parson replies grabbing London by the hand pulling her towards him, "What the hell is this, some kind of mix up? Wait… is this some kind of sick sex slave trade operation?"

"No," Buck yells, "Sit down, both of you!"

"No, I think we'll stand Buck…" London says.

"Fine," Buck says, sitting down on the bed himself, "Your parents paid me a lot of money to take care of you... both of you."

"What the hell," Parson says, "Buck my parents are dead and they died broke. Nobody paid you to keep me. I don't know how I ended up here, but I do know..."

"Nothing," Buck interjects, "You know nothing about life or even yourself, Parson..."

"My parents died broke!" Parson yells.

"Those aren't the parents who paid me," Buck explains, "your real parents did..."

"Wait," London says, "Parson did you just get here today too?"

"Yeah," he replies, "Why?"

"Shut up," Buck says, "Both of you. Now... there's enough money in both of your bank accounts to last you five lifetimes, so it really doesn't matter. Nothing matters."

"Bank account," Parson says laughing uncomfortably, "I've never had a bank account or enough money to put in one in my entire life. And what do you mean *my real parents* paid you to take care of me?"

"Parson," Buck says, "I'd like you to meet your baby sister, London. The specifics of your being lost in the foster care system for so long, and then your parents finally finding you again... I don't have a clue about that son. You will both know everything you desire to know very soon. Until then, just do me a favor and stay alive..."

Stranger things have happened

Or at least that's what people say

Beef stroganoff is my favorite dish

But today is not my favorite day

What about my classmates

What'll they do without me

I'm the most popular kid in school

They only come to school to see me

And hell I'm rich

I should always get my way

Why on Earth I just don't understand

Why my parents would give me away

And now I have a brother

I'm not my parents only born

How do you vanish and leave your children

Without the decency of being warned...

The Strip

"No little girl dreams of growing up to turn out the way I have. This definitely was not a part of the plan but I'm here now and this is life. As I stare into my cloudy smudged bedroom mirror I know full well I have on much more make up than necessary. But then, this is my mask, so it's all very necessary. How else am I supposed to hide all the pain and disgusting memories? I don't deserve to live. I earnestly pissed away every good opportunity I've ever had. I'm damaged and spoiled goods. I allowed bad boys and men to shape my view of the world long ago. I truly

believe that all men are the same. Every guy I ever chose to be with was so obviously bad for me, but that's all I knew and those were the only men I thought I deserved. Now, I'm not even good enough for those scumbags, so I'll just die alone. I'm ready too, whenever it's my time. I honestly don't care if I live or die anymore. Jesus, take the wheel? Hell no, Jesus take my life, I don't want to suffer anymore. I refuse to run back home to my dad. I know he'll help me but I've never felt safe there. When I was about ten years old his friends were the first men to destroy me. Those sick bastards took turns robbing me of my precious adolescent innocence. I don't know if my father knew what was going on or not, but I do know he never did anything about it. It's fine though. It taught me at a very young age that my value lives and dies between my soft milky legs. I'll never be worth anything more than a piece of ass to any man. So since that's all they want, I…"

"Cassie," a raspy voice says from the door way, "girl, are you in here talking to yourself again?"

"Gloria," Cassie replies, "Some people talk to God when they're alone, but God don't give a shit about people like me, so I just talk to myself."

"Whatever, girly…" Gloria says shaking her graying head trying not to wrinkle her old face up too much.

Gloria is fifty-seven years old and she stands about five foot three inches tall. Her once black hair is almost all silver now. She's wearing a short tight dress and lipstick that's way too bright for her age.

"You must be headed out?" Cassie asks.

"Yes ma'am," Gloria replies, "rent ain't gonna pay itself. What time you gonna hit the strip, love?"

"As soon as I figure out which wig to wear..." Cassie admits.

"Okay, well I'll be down below. See you when you come down." Gloria says closing the door behind her as she leaves.

Cassie quickly ties her longish blonde hair up into a bun and then places a red wig on her head just right. Her green eyes are dry and lifeless. She used to be much more attractive than she is now, but when the only men you entertain are men you don't actually want, sooner or later you stop caring how or what you look like.

Ten minutes later, Cassie emerges from the front door of her apartment building. As she walks down the block she's going through her usual silly routines to ready herself for the evening ahead of her.

"I am," Cassie whispers to herself, "Sasha Fierce. I am Sasha Fierce. Every man wants me and every woman wants to be me... I am Sasha Fierce."

As Cassie transforms, each step she takes down the block feels more powerful than the one before. In this moment she is not just a lowly cheap street walker, she's a beautiful, respected queen. She flips her hair and puts a confident hand on her left hip; always the left hip, because that's the diva hip. Nothing can stop her or break her now.

"Aye bitch..." a man says, from the passenger side of a beat up old Honda Civic.

Cassie's diva hand falls down by her side as all her natural insecurities coming rushing back to her conscious.

"Hey baby," Cassie says smiling as she approaches the two men in the car, "you fellas looking for a date?"

"Maybe," the asshole on the passenger side says, "How much?"

"Are you a cop?" Cassie asks.

The passenger smiles back at the driver and then the two men speed away quickly.

"Not tonight," Cassie whispers to herself as she starts back down the block to the strip, "I don't even have enough for rent. I damn sure don't have any bail money."

The strip is flooded every night with all kinds of girls and women. Most of them are over the age of eighteen, but not all of them.

Cassie used to be nervous on the strip since she's one of the only white girls working the area. But now she's much more confident than before, she knows her role well. She sits back and lets all the other girls run up to every car that approaches, and the men who actually want a decent looking white girl will make themselves known to her.

She doesn't have to do as much as most of the other girls to get work, for that, she's thankful. Getting the amount of customers, she normally gets is a gift and a curse. She knows she's putting more miles on her young body than she probably should. But this is her job, and the only way of life she knows, so be it.

De'Lure

Near the edge of the street, Cassie sees a classy black man stepping out of a very expensive car. He's obviously lost. He seems to be asking all the girls for directions to some hotel. Most of the working girls in Vegas aren't actually from Vegas. Cassie was born and raised here in Sin City. She finally approaches the lost and very handsome gentleman.

"Hi…" she speaks to him.

"Well, hello," he replies, "I'm not looking for temporary companionship, but I am looking for a new hotel. My stupid GPS can't find it. Damn phone cost $2,000 and it can't even find the new **Amberella De'Lure Resort Hotel and Casino**."

"Is that where you're staying, sir?" Cassie asks with wide eyes.

"I'm supposed to be," he smiles at her obvious adoration, "But no one knows how to get there."

"I do," Cassie tells him.

"You do…" he replies.

"Yeah," Cassie says, "one of my um… customers did some work on the building. I've been there a couple times; I could take you there."

"I'm sure you can," the man smiles holding a gloved hand out to her, "I'm sorry I didn't catch your name."

"I'm Cassie," she replies, shaking his large strong hand, "and what's your name?"

"Oliver Patton." he tells her.

"**The Oliver Patton**..." Cassie asks.

"You've heard of me?" Mr. Patton asks her.

"Well, no," she blushes, "But with a car like this, and clothes like that, headed to the **Amberella De'Lure Resort Hotel**, I know you must be somebody important."

"Yes I am, my dear," Oliver returns her infectious smile, "Shall we?"

"We shall." Cassie says stepping towards the passenger side of the car.

"What do you think you're doing?" Mr. Patton asks.

"Oh," Cassie blushes again, "I thought... so you just want me to give you the directions right?"

"No, you're taking me," Mr. Patton says, making his way into the passenger side of the luxurious vehicle, "But I want you to drive."

"Hell yes!" Cassie squeals as she makes her way around to the driver's side and quickly hops in the already open door.

As Cassie adjust all the mirrors, she can feel Mr. Patton looking at her.

"You know, Cassie," he croons in his smooth baritone voice, "You don't have to do this."

"Trust me Mr. Patton I'd much rather be in this car with you then out here on this strip all night." Cassie admits.

"No Cassie," he says, looking intently in her eyes, "That's what I mean ... You're very young. I'm sure there's something else you could be doing with your life."

"Don't judge me," Cassie screams, "I enjoy what I do and the money is very good and extremely fast."

"Oh no, ma'am," Patton says, "I'm not judging you at all. See, I used to be a pimp. But after I made about fifty thousand dollars I got clean and went legit. I never looked back."

Looking closer at him, Cassie finds herself getting lost in his passionate eyes. The waves in his hair are very soothing to her soul. His smooth dark chocolate skin is almost hypnotizing, and his voice could make any woman melt instantly.

"Okay captain, save a hoe," Cassie says with a seductive smile, "Can I drive off now or nah, Mr. Patton?"

"Please do," he replies, "But please, call me Oliver."

As they arrive at the hotel just around the corner minutes later, Cassie pulls up to the valet in front of the gigantic hotel. She bashfully looks over at Oliver and smiles.

Oliver laughs to himself. Cassie joins in with his laughter.

"So you mean to tell me that I was this close to the hotel," he asks, "You took *two turns* and we're here..."

"Yes sir," Cassie smiles holding her pale hand out, "Now that'll be $100."

"For what," Oliver says as he wrinkles his brow, "driving me around the corner."

"A girl's gotta eat, Captain Oliver," Cassie smiles.

"Listen," Oliver says reaching in his pocket, "I realize you're white and I'm black, but slavery is long gone and I'm no fool."

"So does that mean you're not going to pay me," she asks, "Because, if you're not going to pay me it's fine. There's nothing I can do about it. You're a man and I'm just a poor hooker. I can't beat the money out of you. I told Gloria I need a pimp. This is why I need a pimp for situations like this. But no… she said. You don't need a pimp, Cassie. He's just going to beat you, control you, and take all your money. Gloria is my roommate, she's been working for over thirty years and she still makes a killing every night. Not bad for an old black broad. Listen, I know I'm rambling, but my rent is due in the morning and if it's not paid I'll…"

"Here's a thousand dollars." Oliver says, handing her ten crisp hundred dollar bills.

"Are you serious, man," Cassie asks, "Now what?"

"Come on," he says stepping out of the car, "You're staying here with me for the weekend."

"You gotta be kidding me." Cassie says, following closely behind the tall handsome man.

"No, I'm not," he replies, "Did you have other plans?"

"Hell no." she smiles.

As they step inside the gorgeous lobby, Cassie nearly loses consciousness from the innate allure of the **Amberella De'Lure Hotel**. The outside of the hotel is unforgettable enough, but the inside all decked out in beautiful bright gold embellishments is almost more than Cassie's awestruck eyes can handle.

Once inside their suite, Oliver picks Cassie up in his arms and carries her to the enormous bed. After he lays her down, he steps back and begins taking off all of his clothes.

"Cassie," he says, "You really don't remember me, do you?"

"No, should I..." she asks.

"Well no not really," Oliver says climbing on top of her, "We went to school together. My being at your strip tonight was no accident. I came looking for you, Cassie. I knew you would be there."

"I don't know who you are, Oliver, but I am glad you showed up tonight." Cassie tells him leaning up off the bed to kiss his strong neck.

"Tenth grade year," Oliver says between kisses, "Your boyfriend and the guy you were cheating on him with, both striped me naked, and beat me to a pulp in front of the entire school."

"Wait," Cassie says, with wide eyes scooting away from the much bigger man, "You're *that* Oliver... the one we used to call..."

"**Oliver Urkel**," he laughs, "Yeah that was me. I graduated at the top of our pitiful class went to college and then went in the military with a very high rank. Now, I buy and sell companies and commercial properties."

"We were so mean to you," Cassie says through shaky lips, "Why would you ever want to help me now?"

"**Help** is such a strong word," Oliver says crawling towards the frightened Cassie, "You see, honestly, I want to… **own** you, **forever**."

"You don't **want** me Oliver, I'm a **prostitute**." Cassie says, trying hard not to have one of her infamous panic attacks.

"On the contrary," he says kissing her on her forehead, "The fact that you're a whore is what turns me on about you the most."

Ghosts from our past lives

Have a way of coming back around

Masked with new faces and old agendas

Designed to destroy our solid ground

We fear no evil

As we walk through the valley of the shadow of death

Instead we accept our known fate

And hold on tight gasping for our own breath

Leave me, no take me

Just try not to break my heart

De'Lure

My life has no value anyway

And there's nothing left of me to fall apart

Walking up and down the strip

I'm lusted after all night

I make men's dreams come true for a second

Then just as quickly they want me out of their sight

My dark knight Oliver has come to save me

Even though he hates me as much as the rest

I'll give him my life if that's what he wants

It's not my fault he settled for less

The Art of Beauty

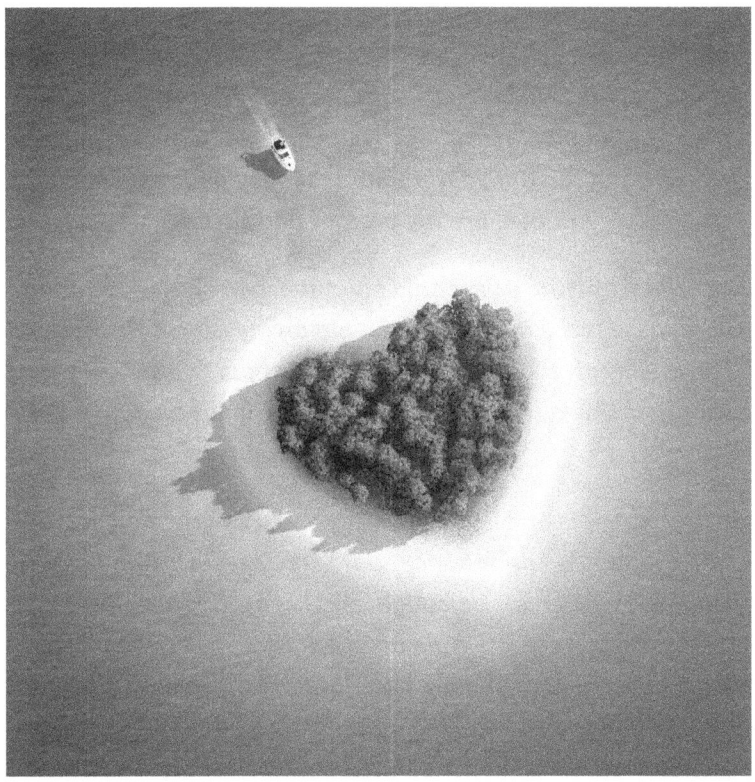

(Prologue)

(Leo)

What is the purpose of contrasting skin colors? Does it determine our self-worth and our social status? Or is it just a natural divider to separate us from those of different ethnic backgrounds? Does the color of my skin even matter? I don't know, but my skin is white and my entire family is black. My mother Tia, the only mother I've ever known named me Leo, after Leonardo DiCaprio her favorite American actor. Fourteen years ago my biological family who are American came here to the Amberella Islands on vacation. From what I was told, while on the island I was kidnapped by ruthless white slave traffickers. Before I could be sold into the slave trade my island mother Tia rescued me, brought me to her home, and raised me as has her own. Her family is the only one I've ever known. Her husband Lex is my father, and their children Kayman and Robyn, are my brother and sister.

When I was twelve years old I met the love of my life Viesha LeCray. She is the most beautiful girl on my island. Her perfect skin is like soft toasted caramel, and her passionate eyes are hazel brown. In the ancient Amberella Islands language her name Viesha, means beauty.

So, this entire Island is owned, yes owned by one man, a crazy old Dr. named Carlos Sanchez. He supposedly lost his mind about ten years ago. He bought this island, and then flew out here on a private jet, and never left. He began building the island up years ago; and the population has tripled in size since then. Half of the Island... the poor half is inhabited by all black people and descendants of the ancient islanders. The other half is gated; I've never been through or to those gates. I've just heard about them since I was a small child.

So I guess I'll tell you a little about me. First and foremost, I'm an exceptional artist. I discovered my passion for the arts at a very young age and now I've grown into quite the painter. I can draw and paint anything, but my favorite subject is Viesha. I've drawn hundreds of portraits of her walking, climbing trees, and even sleeping on a soft blue blanket out on the beach. My bedroom is filled with my pictures of her. She is... the air I breathe.

Chapter 1

The Drinkard's

(14 years before)

Karen Drinkard is the envy of every woman in Charleston, South Carolina. She's devilishly beautiful, sweet as can be, and married to Steven Drinkard the most successful attorney Charleston has ever seen.

The woman just gave birth to their third child, a boy two months ago, and is in better shape than every woman she knows. Her kids worship the very ground she walks on, just like her husband Steve did once upon a time.

Karen is so full of love and life it's just as easy to love her as it is to hate the very sight of her. The woman never seems to have a bad day. And why would she? The home her family resides in is a modern day castle. She drives, wears, and eats only the finest things. From the outside looking in her life couldn't appear any more perfect. The luxurious lifestyle Karen and her husband have built wasn't obtained easily though; they both sacrificed and worked very hard to create it.

Aside from his illustrious legal exploits Steve also owns a line of covenant stores across the south. He has no plans of allowing the rapid growth of his wealth to slow until he's sure his kid's grandkids will be set for life. The man is the ultimate workaholic, but still finds enough time to be a wonderful father and decent husband.

In his mind everything and everyone around him couldn't be any more perfect. He's always prided himself on keeping those close to him happy at all costs. Thus far he has not fallen short too many times.

 Some boys become good men because they watched their seemingly perfect fathers throughout their childhood do so many heroic things like paying bills, cutting grass, and of course holding their mother's hand. Those fathers make it their business to have private moments with their sons to talk to, and teach them about what it means to be a man well before they're old enough to legally drink or drive. These fathers also know the things that they want to instill in their sons won't become a part of them overnight. They understand that grooming and teaching a boy how to be a productive and faithful man is a life long journey and lesson.

This is not the reason Steven Drinkard is an exceptional father. Quite the opposite is true for the aging affluent lawyer. His father David was completely absent throughout his childhood. Steve only saw his father three times as a child, and the third time was in his casket after he finally drank himself to death.

At twelve years old, young Stevie as they called him back then stood in front of his mother's small church and sang a verse of the popular country hit "Whiskey Lullaby". By that age little Stevie had already mastered the art of sarcasm. A shocked hush fell over the entire church after the boy finished his impressive rendition of the popular song. That night alone in his room he prayed and cursed God en route to promising himself he would never be anything like his father. He held true to that promise.

Chapter 2

"Karen"

Sitting alone in the back of her enormous walk-in closet little miss sunshine is staring into her large lighted vanity mirror. As she looks into her own piercing blue eyes she's trying to figure out why she even wears makeup at all. She's not an arrogant woman but she does realize she's just as pretty now naturally as she's ever been with makeup on.

She involuntarily shakes her long dirty blond hair as a lone tear falls down her smiling face.

"Steven…" she whispers aloud to the lonely closet walls, *"I love you very much… I appreciate everything you've ever done for me and our children. Our children are so precious and perfect in your eyes… I love our children just as much as you do, maybe even more because I gave birth to them, but I can't help but feel like with every child we bring into this world some of your love for me is stolen and then transferred from me to them. My God, am I talking to myself again? I'm such a coward! No I'm not, I am not a coward, I'm just a respectable woman, and I know what expressing these sentiments to my husband would entail… Steve would never understand this pain."*

"Karen…" the strong voice calls from the bedroom door.

She quickly dries her reddened face and tries to gain some composure. The closet door opens.

"Honey…" the voice says getting closer by the second.

"I'm in here Steve." Karen says gently.

"Well there you are honey;" he smiles down at his gorgeous wife; "Jamie and Jason are looking for you downstairs."

Karen can't help but notice how handsome her husband is. The man seems to get so much better physically with every passing year. His dark brown hair is combed and trimmed perfectly in perfect contrast with his slightly unkempt beard that gives him the rough look he's grown to like lately. His hazel-green eyes are just as genuine in this moment as they were the very first time she lost herself in them as a girl so long ago.

"Karen..." Steve says noticing her staring at him.

"I'm sorry... please tell the kids I'll be down in a minute." Karen smiles back at him.

"Karen," Steve bends down close to her face, "Were you crying just now? Yes, yes you were, don't shake your head honey... What's wrong darlin' did the kids do something, because I'll get on their little behinds right damn now..."

Steve turns to leave in pursuit of his children.

"No," Karen calls out as the tears begin to flood her face again, "It's not the kids Steven."

"It's not," he makes his way back to her, "then darlin' what is it, whatever you want done, you know I can do it baby."

"No," she stares deep into his eyes, "I don't think you can this time darlin'."

"What's this about Karen," he kneels down beside her with her left hand in his, "Now honey you're scaring me. If it's something I did just tell me so I'll never do it again?

In the room connected to their master bedroom Karen and Steve can hear their new born son crying out at the top of his tiny lungs.

"Hold that thought honey," Steve says turning to leave again, "I'll be right back, and I want you to tell me what it is I'm doing wrong love."

"That…" she whispers to herself as her husband rushes off to coddle their newborn son yet again.

As Karen stares back deep into her large mirror she can sense something very dark behind her eyes, she can feel her body and heart growing very cold. As her body begins to shake uncontrollably she grabs hold of the dresser supporting her mirror to steady herself. After inhaling and exhaling deeply several times Karen can feel herself regaining some sanity about her.

 In the distant behind her in the mirror's reflection she can see expensive boxes of shoes piled almost to the ceiling in her dimly lit closet. Color coded rows of designer clothing are flowing and weaving all around her closet like a mind blowing abstract oil painting created just for her. As she looks at all the things her husband and their life together have afforded her she can't help but to start crying again.

"Money is great," she whimpers, "It really is, it makes life so much more full and easy, but it can't save my heart and it can't make me happy… not anymore. I know that this closet contains articles of clothing from every major and some private designers all over the world, all three of my cars are some of the rarest foreign vehicles ever assembled, and my

home is perfection... but all of it, all of this is just stuff. I just want my husband back, and all to myself."

Chapter 3

"All Aboard"

The night air is cool but comforting as it brushes past the Drinkard family. Steve is leading the way holding the hands of his young son and daughter Jason and Jamie. A few steps behind them is his gorgeous wife Karen carrying her new born son wrapped delicately and tighter than necessary in a soft blue and yellow blanket.

As she walks she can't take her eyes off the infant's curious blue eyes staring back up into hers. She's smiling at him, but the sentiments don't feel real, they haven't for a few days now.

"All aboard..." an older white gentleman yells from near the ships loading area. The Drinkard's sleepily make their way onto the huge luxurious cruise ship in pursuit of their rooms for a good night's sleep.

After tucking his two older kids in their beds, Steve makes his way back into his suite that connects to their room. In the middle of their huge bed he finds his infant son Jeremiah fast asleep. Karen is staring in the mirror as if she's waiting on it to say something to her. Steve wants to say something to her but he thinks better of it and instead climbs up into the enormous bed next to his tiny son.

Karen turns to look at him.

"Of course..." she mumbles.

"What?" Steve yawns without moving.

"I said of course." Karen stares back into the mirror, trying to find at least a piece herself.

"Of course what Karen," Steve sits up, "What is the problem now hunny?"

"Of course." she ignores his question.

"Of course what woman," Steve stands up from the bed, "Are you losing your damn mind?"

"I might be damn it," she yells, "You walk your inconsiderate behind back in here..."

"Now wait a minute *darlin'*, now I can tell you're upset..." Steve walks closer to her.

"Oh can you," she smiles harshly, "Well *congratufuckinlations* oh brilliant lawyer. Yes, I am upset... I *hate* you, and I *hate* the fact that our children matter more to you than me!"

"That is not true honey," Steve attempts to stand her up, "Tell me what's really wrong, where is all this crazy talk coming from?"

"I just told you Steven," she pulls away from him harshly, "And stop with all of those stupid pet names, I never liked them! You spend time with our kids every day and I get whatever's left of you at the end of the day. You haven't touched me but twice in the past three years."

"Now that's just not true Karen." Steve turns his back in disbelief of what he's hearing.

"No you don't," Karen stands up and pushes Steve hard in his back, "You do not turn your back on me! Don't you ever turn your back on me!"

"Woman, have you lost your mind?" Steve steps face to face with her.

"Apparently," Karen grand stands, "I think we've established that I've lost *my* mind. *I'm* the crazy one, something has to be wrong with Karen… *good ole faithful Mrs. fucking Drinkard!* What about *Mr.* Drinkard? *Hmm*, what's wrong with him? Or is he just as perfect as *everyone outside* of his marriage *thinks* he is? You are perfect aren't you honey bun?"

"No one is perf…" Steve starts.

"*No one is perfect*," Karen interjects, "*of fucking course!* You always say the perfect robotic *predictable* generic response to *everything*! Why… how did we become that couple?"

"*What couple* Karen, who is it that you think we've become, because honestly at this point I don't know *who* the hell we are?" Steve gently grabs her face.

"Well at least you're admitting we have no identity together," Karen quickly removes his cold hands from her face, "your hands feel like ice."

"I'm sure they do, stuck in this room with a bitter nagging insufferable bitch!" Steve angrily makes his way back to the bed.

"Did you just call me a bitch Steven?" Karen walks towards him.

"I'm sorry Karen…" he looks up into her eyes from the foot of the bed.

"**No**," Karen yells, "Do not apologize! **That's good**, **this** is **good** and **natural**. We can fight; we're **supposed** to fight sometimes! That's what **married** people who love each other do. But **instead** we're this dry, methodical, robotic imaginary couple from some corny white magazine cover."

The door to the joint sweet opens.

"Mama, Daddy…" their daughter Jamie looks at them both with her mother's big bright blue eyes.

"Oh honey…" Steve stands up.

Karen quickly pushes him back down to the bed.

"Jamie, go lay back down and go to sleep." Karen turns her around and closes the door behind her.

"**You're sick**…" Steve growls.

"Am I…" she yells.

"Yes," Steve replies, "you are very sick!"

"No you're just weak Steven!" Karen stalks towards him quickly.

"Weak…" he looks up into her eyes again.

"Hell yes," Karen confirms, "**Every** man in our church, **every** one of your golf buddies, and even your little brother Darryl wants to have sex with me. You are married to **the** sexiest woman in

De'Lure

Charleston, South Carolina and you *never* even touch me. I don't know if you're *gay* or…"

"Damn it Karen!" Steve stands up to face her.

"Does it even work anymore?" she smiles a devilish smile as she gropes his crotch.

Steve pushes her back from him.

"My brother does not want to have sex with you Karen, now you take that back!" Steve demands.

Karen laughs in his face with no regard for his feelings.

"You know what Steven," she smiles again, "You're right Darryl doesn't want to have sex with me… *anymore*. You see, he told me it was just a fantasy of his. I guess one time was good enough… *and he loved it*…"

Karen steps closer to her red faced teary eyed husband and gropes his crotch again.

"I have to admit," she whispers, "I'd trade every time we've ever had sex to just feel Darryl inside me *one more time*…"

Whap!!!

Steve slaps Karen down to the floor.

"*You evil bitch*!" he cries out from the depths of his pained throat…

"*My brother*, Karen…" Steve kneels down over her.

"Why not," Karen scoots away from him, "*He* wanted me *you* didn't…"

"You're a very sick woman Karen…" Steve shakes his head.

Karen pulls her gown over her blonde head and throws it on the floor behind her. Looking deep in Steve's eyes she lays back on the floor spread eagle. Her perfect nude body is glowing in the dim light for him to gaze upon.

"Karen what the hell…" Steve growls.

"Come here baby…" she moans.

"Suddenly I'm not in the mood." Steve stands up and turns to head to the bathroom still wiping away new tears.

"**Suddenly,**" Karen laughs, "**You're a coward Steven Drinkard**… You **can't** handle me; I'm too good for you. I always have been."

Steve stops dead in his tracks.

"Karen," he doesn't bother to looks back at her, "**I love you** very much… but at some point I lost a **big** part of your respect and admiration for me. How can I ever be a man with a woman like what you've become?"

Steve walks into the bathroom closing the door behind him.

"See," Karen screams, "You can't even screw me anymore, the only time you can is when you're trying to bring another one of these despicable, little attention whore, bastards into the world!"

Karen stands up in her nakedness and pounces on the huge bed waking her sleeping child up. She looks down into his pretty little sleepy blue eyes. After clearing her throat to collect as much mucus as she possibly can she spits in his tiny face. Baby Jeremiah starts crying immediately.

De'Lure

Then with all her might Karen begins choking the life out of him stopping his cries in his tiny throat.

The bathroom door flies open. Karen quickly picks the baby, wipes the slimy spit from his face as best she can, puts her left nipple in his mouth, and then rocks him close to her body.

"Karen…" Steve walks towards the bed.

"What, he was hungry," she lies, "**What**… do you want to breast feed them now too Mr. Mom?"

(The following poem is about the actual protagonist of the full length version of this story)

"The Art of Beauty"

Painting your life on my canvas

Is a blessing in itself

A beauty like yours transcends all things

Your love is vital to my health

From the moment my eyes

Drowned inside yours

My mind was ever numb

And my soul began to soar

High above any understanding I possess

You created in me new life

You even took and changed a bachelor's heart

And forced me to consider taking a wife

I dream of you often

I paint pictures of your body in my mind

Your hypnotizing curves

Firm thighs and soft behind

The windows to your soul

Two gorgeous orbs of brown

Your lips and tongue when you speak my name

There'll never be a more pleasant sight or sound

In this life obstacles come and go

But destiny always win

For as long as I'm still on this earth

You'll embody my beginning and end

Passion Absolute

Radicon's Princess

(Prologue)

Miami, Florida is located on the Atlantic coast in southeastern Florida and the county seat of Miami-Dade County. It's no secret how exciting the city of Miami is from sun up, to sun down, and beyond. Sex, drugs, and money bursts from every single street corner and establishment. You can get married, laid, high, or killed all on the same block. You can become a millionaire or you can die broke and alone in a cold dark gutter.

Love exists everywhere, and every being at some point is capable of loving another being. In Miami though it's a lot harder to know and distinguish real love from carefully calculated deceit-filled pseudo affection. This is true especially among the elite. There are so many seemingly beautiful, successful people of all kinds of backgrounds, its damn near impossible to tell if someone is actually who and what they say they are.

3185 Dunbarton Lane has been the home address of the extremely wealthy Radicon clan for forty plus years. Old man Raymond Radicon had the estate built from the ground up in 1971 when he was just twenty-one years old. His father Dorian Radicon was a simple man, very affluent as well but he was complacently satisfied with the uncomplicated things in life. Dorian could have built a home equally as grand as the palace Ray had built on Dunbarton Lane, but he wanted his money to last generations and not to be squandered off on expensive meaningless things.

Ch. 1

"Night Rider"

The night air is wafting in through the car window gently bathing both of their warm bodies with a calming breeze. The air in Miami is so sweet, it opens you up to so many amazing possibilities that you would have never even considered before.

The unlikely couple is riding along the strip quietly without a care in the world. Well, at least he is. She's lost deep in her heart's desires as she ponders her inner most thoughts. There is real beauty to be found in that anxious moment when you hope, and ultimately think the person sitting right next to you feels exactly the same way you feel.

Not that you actually want to know the answer, because there's always that chance that you're all alone in your fantasy love connection. But that's the beauty of love, isn't it? It's you stepping out on faith and taking chances; showing someone pieces of you that the rest of the world isn't usually privy to see. You can't delve into a potential love with training wheels on, that's the fastest and surest way to crash.

You have to be open and insane when it comes to love. If he or she is really worth your time, don't be afraid to let that person know you're open to them and their way of thinking. Be very careful about that. Carolyn is sure she has everything under control with Mr. Radicon.

On the radio Mariah Carey is singing her 90's hit, "My All". This is one of Carolyn's favorite songs of all time. As a young teen she used to believe in everlasting love that could never grow dull and useless.

Then she got married to *him*, and realized a love like that only truly exists in fairytales. Or maybe not... Real love she thinks, with the right person, and in the right circumstance can be sustained far longer than her personal situation.

Her personal situation could end right now, this very second and she'd probably be happier. Being alone would be a major upgrade as opposed to being with her husband.

Carolyn Olivier is only twenty-three years young and she's been married every day since her 19th birthday. The wedding was small but cozy. Her parents came ahead of time, but his parents were late.

They're always late for everything, but somehow they always have the most to say. Carolyn's just glad her in-laws finally moved away. Her father-in-law Greg Olivier got a management job at a car dealership in Orlando which caused him and his wife to move away two years ago.

His wife Marilyn, her husband's mother is a professional church member. She's one of those women who are at church **every single time** the door's open. She's in every choir, every program, and has to speak at every function.

It makes you wonder, how fucked up she must have been in the past, that she's working overtime just to make herself believe she's saved and forgiven. However; in the event of raising their son, they did a terrible job.

He definitely tricked Carolyn, and ultimately guilted her into saying yes to his lofty marriage proposal four years ago. He told her she was never going to find any man that was going to be faithful to her, love her unconditionally, and be man enough to marry her.

She believed him; maybe he was right. After all she was only eighteen, who the hell finds true lasting love at eighteen anymore?

Ultimately she married him on her nineteenth birthday, and became a slave to a dry, monotonous, robotic, lifestyle. The type of lifestyle that plagues so many marriages across the globe today.

At first she just endured it believing that her life was just the way marriage were supposed to be. Then she started smoking, and smoking turned into drinking. Neither habit lasted long because she had never been the type to stick with anything too long good or bad, including substance abuse.

Next she started buying overtly erotic novels by the bundle, mommy porn as they call it.

She also owns an impressive arsenal of sex toys that she hides in the drawers of her nightstand on her husband's side of the bed. Of course he has never found them or noticed; just like he doesn't notice anything else she does for that matter.

Honestly she was hoping he'd find her dirty little toys, and that maybe finding them would spark his interest and imagination and make him want to start exploring with her sexually. They could begin a new erotic journey together and send their humdrum marriage down a new blossoming golden path of eternal orgasmic explosions.

But of course he never noticed her toys, and if he did he never bothered to mention to her that he had. Oh God, the man is so boring and predictable it's almost comical. Carolyn once had a ridiculous pink streak dyed down the back of her hair just to see if he would notice it. He did, a month later while he was giving her some routine mediocre sex from behind.

It's always from behind with him, she wonders if he's maybe no longer attracted to her, and in turn prefers to have sex with her from the back so that he can imagine she's someone else. This wouldn't bother her at all. In fact, for the past two and a half years the only way Carolyn has felt any pleasure with her husband, is to imagine during sex that he's some stranger she met on the street, fucking her in a random alley for cash.

She relies on her extremely vivid imagination, because that's the only way the poor woman can feel even an ounce of pleasure for the five minutes he humps her quickly from behind once or twice a week.

Four years and two kids later her body is screaming for some much needed excitement. Carolyn has grown even more beautiful with each passing year. Along with her beauty, her painful unhappiness has grown as well.

Carolyn is 5'4, sinfully curvaceous, with hazel eyes, and toasted caramel skin. Her long brown hair is pulled back into a tight ponytail tonight. She can't see a thing as he blindfolded her tightly the second she got inside his expensive vehicle. She's wearing a gorgeous yellow fitted body dress that he made her change into moments ago.

To change into the dress, she got completely naked as he drove down a crowded Miami street never knowing if anybody driving near them saw her nude body or not. But she knows he doesn't care. If anyone did see her perfect naked body, that probably turned him on even more.

James Radicon, the son of Raymond Radicon is the richest man in Miami, Florida. His late father left him everything he had in the world in his last will and testament. And by everything I do mean an eternal fortune.

The origin of the Radicon's wealth was unknown even to old man Ray Radicon his entire life. All he knew is he was born rich because of his father before him and he was going to die rich, just like his grandfather did. James on the other hand is close to unveiling the true secret behind his family's age old fortune.

"Where are we going James?" Carolyn asks finally breaking the silence.

"Shut up." he replies blankly. Carolyn tries to sneakily readjust her blindfold so she can sneak a glimpse of their current location. James quickly looks over at her.

"Bitch if I so much as see either one of your eyes you're gonna get it. Her hands fall helplessly back down to her lap. "Well where are we going James?" she asks again. He doesn't respond.

She exhales abruptly trying to pretend she's angry. She can barely sit still riding next to this man. She's wanted him for as long as she can remember. She had never been noticeably attracted to white men before him, and she knows after him the attraction will most likely cease to exist.

James Radicon stands six feet two inches tall, with an impressive athletic body shape. His blond hair is exquisite and always trimmed to perfection. His nose is small and narrow but distinct. His ears are not too big and not too small they're adorable just as cute as he is. His blue eyes are absolutely hypnotic and they fit his face to classical perfection. The man has never known rejection in his adult life. His sinfully sensual eyes have never failed him they always close the deal.

"Damn it James, just tell me where we're going!" Carolyn yells, forgetting momentarily just how dangerous James Radicon really is. He looks towards her smiling sadistically at her blind face, and her weak attempt at bravado.

"Tonight all your fantasies become instant reality once again my dear." he promises in a grandiose tone.

"My fantasies," Carolyn scoffs, "I'm allowed to have those? I thought only your fantasies mattered."

"Shut the fuck up Carolyn," Mr. Radicon fumes, "what deeper fantasy could any bitch ever possess other than satisfying me? I am *your* God, never forget that!"

"Some God." she turns her head. James quickly reaches over and slaps her hard across the mouth. She doesn't speak. Instead she just wisely holds her throbbing mouth in complete fear and silence.

"Now we're almost here," he looks at her, "do not embarrass me."

"Yes sir." she mumbles meekly.

"You will speak only when spoken to and do exactly as you are told," he grabs her right knee gently; "if I do not object to something you are told to do... you will not object either." "Yes sir Mr. Radicon." she mumbles again.

James parks his expensive SUV on the street near the deserted looking mansion. "Hell, I might as well go first." he smiles to himself.

He unzips his tight jean pants. She knows exactly what that sounds means for her. Carolyn seductively wets her voluptuous lips with an anxious smile plastered on her beautiful light brown face. James loves her lips almost as much as he loves her behind.

As he grabs her ponytail, she readies herself mentally for the oncoming oral intrusion. He holds her head just close enough to it so she can lick the tip thoroughly just the way he likes it. Then she begins to take him deep in her mouth and throat. His eyes are closed and his mouth is wide open. Suddenly there's a knock on his SUV window.

"What the hell..." James jumps.

"The Master said bring her inside immediately." the masked man tells Radicon. Radicon nods. Then the masked man turns and makes his way back up the hill to the dark mansion.

Carolyn continues to service him with no hands. James has trained her perfectly. Looking down at her he can't quite figure out how to make her stop. He realizes she's enjoying this even more so than he is.

"Let's go." Radicon tells her finally. She doesn't stop. Her wet hungry mouth just can't tear itself away from him.

James pulls her ponytail as hard as he possibly can, ultimately ripping himself, out of her lustful oral grasp. Carolyn is in sudden pain from her head down to her neck. As she caresses her own shoulders and neck silently she is relieved that the hair in her ponytail was her real hair, because had it been a weave Radicon would have surely snatched it right out of her head.

James opens his door and steps out calmly, and then begins brushing his clothes off as he notices a few pieces of lint on his tight black V-neck shirt. After peeling each piece off, he makes his way around to her side of the truck. He opens her door and takes her by the hand. She hesitates now.

"Wait James," she whispers, "I can't see." she complains.

106

"Of course you can't see you, *idiot*, that's the whole point of the damn blindfold." he tells her.

"Geez Carolyn," he continues, "you're already black, please don't continue to say stupid things like that... It's so expected." She doesn't respond.

Using his hand to find her balance she carefully steps down out of the SUV. "Lead the way." she tells him.

As they make their way up the hill Radicon finds his adrenaline pumping through him fiercely. He so loves these random late night rendezvous. He has been a student of the Master for quite some time now, and he lives in his large shadow. Radicon only breathes to learn more and more about the art of sexual pain and pleasure.

As they approach the large stained glass door Radicon smiles at the genius of its design. He has seen and walked through the exquisite door many times before but tonight its detail is screaming for his undivided attention.

In the center most part of the door is the Virgin Mary holding the precious baby Jesus, standing in front of an upside down five-point star, with red rose petals all around their feet. In the air flying all around and above their heads are beautiful winged angels and demons battling for their souls, or at least this is Radicon's interpretation of the art piece.

He does know that the Master is absolutely obsessed with the book and movie "The Da Vinci Code" so the occult symbolism James suspects in the door's art is very real.

As he and the still silent Carolyn enter the Master's mansion he feels a very real chill come over his body. He should be used to it all by now, but whenever he's in the presence of his mentor his body always goes through real changes that he can't help but to feel.

Radicon kneels down close to Carolyn and removes both of her shoes from her tiny feet. Then he stands back up and begins leading the gorgeous young woman towards her unchosen fate for the evening.

"James..." Carolyn whispers. He spins around and slaps her hard across her mouth again. "Bitch you only speak when you are spoken to." he reminds her.

As they near the entrance to the large living room Carolyn's entire body has caught a chill because of the ice cold marble floor beneath her unsure feet. Music begins to play. It seems to be an old "112" song from an album that Carolyn can't quite remember the name of.

(Carolyn)

I want nothing more than to be this man's deepest fantasy. I owe him that much, because he is already my deepest fantasy. His voice, his lips, his regal eyes...damn it the way he walks carrying with him the absolute perfection that he calls his body. His confidence bleeds through honestly via his impeccable style and swagger.

I will do anything he asks of me. I could... No I should be his one and only wife, and not just his, his submissive whore. But I would be this creation he has fashioned me into, and do the freaky sometimes near unbearable things he makes me do until I stop breathing... Just to be near him.

I don't deserve his time; he shouldn't even know my name or that I even exist. Because he made me, I was not really alive until he awakened me mind body and spirit. Of all the wonderful and at time subpar lovers he has afforded and or force upon me in the past six months he is still by far the best lover I have ever had the pleasure of being used by.

The only man who may top James is the man he calls the Master. James seems to worship this man whom I've never actually seen, but I feel like the Master is always near me when I'm with James because everything we do together seems to at some point have been planned or mandated by the Master himself. The Master is supposed to be some kind of sex genius...

"And who is this delicious dark dish?" a deep raspy voice inquires as they reach the room that connects to the huge living room.

"How are you, this evening Master," Radicon asks, "and this my friend is Carolyn Olivier one of my... more special pieces."

James studies the Master's face carefully like he always does. The old man's face isn't pretty to say the least. The Master isn't an ugly man, but he does look like he was in a terrible accident and had to have his face surgically reconstructed.

"And special she is my son," the Master replies, "tell me James, why is it exactly that you are subjecting such a gorgeous specimen to my unorthodox brand of entertainment?"

De'Lure

James looks at Carolyn for a moment, and then squints, his eyes as he looks at her from head to toe.

"She's beautiful," Radicon agrees, "but I have no room in my life to realistically fall for any woman. It's all just a game... Right Master it's all just a game we play, and in turn bless a select few to join and enjoy our brand of entertainment?"

"So," the Master says, "you're telling me that you have no value for, or recollection of what true love is?"

"Absolutely none at all," Radicon claims, "sex and love have no true value in this world. Once people realize that, they open themselves up to the opportunity of being a lot more successful in life as a whole."

The Master smiles a knowing smile.

"How so son?" the Master asks. Radicon doesn't reply.

"No, please explain James." the Master insists.

"Sir we are getting way off track here, we should all be jumping Ms. Olivier like hungry horny dogs by now." Radicon laugh nervously.

"In due time," the Master points towards the girl giving two of his masked men some sort of signal, "how is it that you a married man put no value in love?" the Master asks. "I learned from my father." Radicon replies coldly.

The two masked men escort the blindfolded Carolyn towards the Master. Now that she is standing right in front of him, he explores her face thoroughly and the curves of her explosive young body. With his left hand he begins to lift her skirt slowly.

She doesn't resist. With a hand on each thigh he prompts her to spread her legs more. She obeys the obvious instruction. The bottom of her new tight yellow body dress is now resting atop her soft round caramel behind.

The Master grabs hold of her soft wet center as if to check her pulse. With his right hand on her stomach and his left hand groping her vagina he begins to wildly massage her throbbing wetness. Her moans are delightful.

James closes his eyes in the distance as the sounds of her pleasure wash over his joyous ears like the soft tones of an angel's voice.

"Master…" she moans.

"Yes Carolyn." he replies. "Do what you will, to me…" she cries impatiently. "Oh I am," he smiles, "trust me my dear your ass belongs to me… at least for tonight."

The Master glances over at James to check his facial expression. Just as he thought the look on James' at this point face isn't quite one of jealousy but it's not exactly one of pleasure either.

"Come close son." the Master says with his smile still completely intact. Radicon obeys. Standing by the Master's side he can't take his eyes off of the beautiful entranced black woman before him.

De'Lure

The mystery of the Master's touch is all James can think about. Carolyn seems to thoroughly enjoy the sex they have together, but the noises she's making now have never graced his corner office, the utility closet during his daily lunch break, of the back seat of any of his luxury vehicles.

What is this? I'm not jealous, I can't be jealous. I am the son of Raymond Radicon. I can literally screw any woman I want. There has never been one woman, in my adult life that I've wanted to fuck that I haven't. I'm perfect. So why now would I be... How could I possibly be jealous over this little black employee of mine? I mean sure she has a great ass and she's not bad to look at, okay she's perfect. But, she's just a part of my fantasy she doesn't really exist to me.

The room is very well lit. The Master insist on the lighting to be as such because his eyes aren't what they used to be and he always says more than anything he enjoys watching. The two masked men are shirtless and covered in oil, wearing black leather pants, and black combat boots.

The Master motions for one of the masked men to come near to him. The man begins carefully stripping her clothes from her throbbing wet body. She's soaked with sweat, and passion. She could have never imagined being this fully aroused in a room full of strange men.

(Hours later)

As they pull up to the small brick house on the corner of Jefferson Street, it appears to look just the way it did when James picked Carolyn up hours ago. Not one light on inside the home. James parks his SUV just across the street from the house. Carolyn staring out of the passenger window towards her house hesitates to exit the vehicle.

"Is something wrong baby girl?" Radicon asks in genuine concern. She looks at him, but she remains silent.

"Hey," he starts, "if what happened back there was too much..."

"I loved it." she interjects.

"I love pleasing you James," she continues, "the passion and intrigue on your perfect face and the look in your enchanting eyes was enough to will me to do almost anything."

James isn't sure how to respond. He wrinkles his left brow, and then gently clears his dry throat so that he can attempt to speak. "But Carolyn," he starts, "you have a husband I'm just you're..."

"A husband," she starts, "in my mind at least... is a man who possesses a woman's mind first, then her body, and then finally her spirit. A woman's true husband is the man she pheens for constantly, the one she dreams about. You, James Radicon embody all of my sweetest dreams and I wake up every single morning wishing it was you lying next to me."

James turns around to look out of the driver's side window. He wipes some warm sweat from his forehead, clears his throat again and begins scratching the top of his well-kept blond head.

"It's um... Very late Carolyn," he mumbles, "you should get inside before he..."
She opens her door and steps out of his truck. She immediately looks down and tries to straighten her soiled yellow gown.

De'Lure

Before walking away, she turns back to look at him with an awkward grin on her face.

"I may be just a fool to you Mr. Radicon," she says, "but what wife doesn't play the fool sometimes? Goodnight James."

She closes the door and makes her way towards her house where she lives with Ralph, her actual legal husband of four years now. James drives off into the distance, all the while secretly watching her in his rear view mirror to ensure she makes it inside the house safely.

Once she's inside he readjusts his mirror and sets his mind on what may be possibly waiting on him when he gets home himself.

Before retiring to her room she takes a left in the front room towards her children's room. She opens their door quietly and tip toes in completely undetected. She finds her three-year-old Ralph Jr. sleeping quietly in his Spider-Man bed. She smiles down at him as she makes her way to her 11 month old Karan's crib. Looking down at his tiny angelic face she's in awe. She feels as if she's being showered with love as her eyes find themselves lost in the perfect design of his adorable face. Her son's beauty has washed away the memory and the sins of the lustful evening she just encountered.

She bends down to pick him up, and then she kisses him gently. After laying him back down safely in his little crib she turns around to find Ralph Jr. smiling up at her.

"Hey mommy..." he whispers.

"Hey Mama's baby." she whispers back returning his infectious smile. The three year olds smile quickly fades into a sad frown.

"I miss you, mommy," he tells her, "you don't love me and Karan anymore." the toddler begins to cry. Carolyn quickly picks him up in her soft arms.

"No, no baby, don't cry," she tells him, "you're my big boy."

"You don't love me Mama." he cries.

"Don't say that Junior." she tells him.

"You never come home and play with me no more mommy." he tells her crying harder with each painful syllable.

Carolyn picks her older son up high in the air so that he is face to face with her. "Baby," she says, "I do love you. Mommy just has a lot going on at work. But you know what…"

"What…" he whines?

"Mommy is going to leave work early tomorrow," Carolyn tells her son, "and come straight home and play with you *all* the way until it's time for your bath."

"What about my baby brother?" the three-year-old asks.

"Of course baby," she smiles at his adorable serious demeanor, "I'm going to play with you and your baby brother. Now little boy it's time for you to go to sleep… Okay?"

"Okay mommy." Ralph Jr. grins.

She kisses him on the lips three times and then tucks him safely back in his Spider-Man bed. Then Carolyn leaves their room and heads towards her own.

De'Lure

Back inside her bathroom Carolyn walks solemnly to her large window that looks out across her nice sized back yard.

"Is this my choice," she whispers, "is anything in my control? Or am I just trapped in this man's fantasy until he decides he's finally finished with me? I'm far from stupid, I've seen "The Family that Preys" I know James Radicon will never be my husband... But even still the rush I get just from being in his presence feels much better than anything I've ever felt with Ralph. Lord I guess these rambling words of mine are some kind of sick prayer. When you pray you have to ask for something right? But I don't know exactly what it is I want or need. Yes, I do... make me white Lord. Please God just make me white so I can be good enough to be James' wife, I don't want to struggle with Ralph anymore in this tiny house. Damn it. Poor Ralph and I know how much he loves me. If he ever found out about this, he would..."

Carolyn shakes her head nervously as she makes her way to her bathroom mirror. Looking at her reflection, she has no clue who this woman is staring back at her. She sees a black whore who would do anything and everything to satisfy a man who could never righteously marry her. The bags under her weary eyes are bold or at least they seem that way to her.

The makeup that's left on her face looks absolutely atrocious. She looks to herself like an ugly old dark clown waiting to pop out from behind a tattered old curtain to perform in front of some cheap circus crowd.

And oh God her breath, she can still taste and smell all four men on her own breath and her entire body is still throbbing in both pain and pleasure.

She grabs her tooth brush and an old tube of Colgate toothpaste. She covers the brush with a generous amount of tooth paste and then begins brushing her teeth vigorously.

After she rinses her mouth out after brushing her teeth she stares back in the mirror again. Her hair is a mess. Her tight ponytail didn't last ten minutes after the evening's festivities began. Her brown curls are all over her head stretched out from being tugged and snatched back and forth for hours.

Carolyn turns around and approaches her lonely shower. She leans on the glass door of it as she turns it on. In her mind she can't help but ponder all the secrets only her bathroom walls know about her inner most thoughts and sentiments.

She smiles, but not for long as she turns back towards her mirror the warm tears begin to storm her pain-filled face like never before. "God I don't want to be a fool forever. Lord, please save me from my own mind." she cries silently.

After a long steaming hot shower Carolyn finally steps out of her almost clean tub onto the bathroom floor. The tile floor is uncomfortable to her touch. All of the bathroom rugs are in the laundry room on the floor where they've been for about eight days now.

The rugs are stuck there because neither she nor Ralph, have been considerate enough to take a moment to go in there and actually wash them. This would be the first time their dingy orangish bath rugs have ever been washed in over three years. The only reason they were going to wash them now is because one of their children threw up all over their bathroom over a week ago.

De'Lure

With a towel she found hanging on the back of her bathroom door Carolyn begins to dry the excess water off of her beautiful, drained, naked body. After sliding into her old purple bath robe she uses a towel from the bathroom closet to dry her wild hair.

With her robe on and a towel wrapped carefully around her head she opens the bathroom door. Standing there staring into her bedroom Carolyn is forced to think about how different her life would be if she was Mrs. James Radicon and not just Mrs. Ralph Olivier.

Looking at her queen sized bed she sees him lying there sound asleep. He doesn't seem to have a care in the world. And he doesn't, he has his pretty little trophy wife, a dead end factory job, a car and a home. He's content.

At twenty-four years old Ralph Olivier has the body of a forty-year-old man. He was never a very physically fit man, but the past four years he really let himself go. He's dark skinned and he wears his hair in a low buzz cut with a silly childish part cut in the side of his plain head.

Everything about him is plain, his face, his walk, even the things he says. He's just a dull guy. Ralph stands about 5'7 and he wears the same three or four outfits year round.

Carolyn is well aware that he prides himself on the fact that she, his wife is prettier than all of his friend's wives and girlfriends. If only he knew his wife was in love with and sleeping with another man. What's more, Ralph actually had the audacity to cheat on her first. He's cheated on Carolyn and gotten caught multiple times over the span of their four-year marriage.

That's part of the reason Carolyn didn't even pretend to be resisting her bosses' sexual advances once they became more obvious.

As Carolyn walks towards the bed her heart is pounding in her chest. Not because she fears or cares what Ralph might think anymore, but because she's can't get the Master and his men out of her mind. The things they did to her, the things James let them do to her were extraordinary.

She would have stayed there in that creepy old house forever if James would have allowed it. She would have lived there forever chained to a bed in one of the Master's many bedrooms completely nude waiting to satisfy any takers. James has awakened in her an inner sexual goddess that she never even knew could exist.

As she lies down next to her husband she continues to mentally relive the evenings many pleasures. Ralph instinctively rolls over close to her in his sleep and wraps his hairy dark arms around her. She cringes at the smell of his natural body odor. It's nothing new; he's always had that smell, even fresh out of the shower his smell remains. She closes her eyes to endure yet another night trapped in his unsuspecting arms.

Chapter 2
"Doughnuts and Tea"

The sun is shining in brightly through the large window in the master bedroom. The trees outside the window are filled with happy birds singing praises to the clouds. James wishes they would all just shut up. He's never been anything close to a morning person. But for some reason this morning as he rolls over and detaches his cell phone from its charger he has a real smile on his face.

The text message on his screen reads, "good morning sir can I do anything to make your morning better?" He covers his head with one of his large fluffy white pillows to hide his obvious happiness.

"She actually does wake up thinking about me." he mumbles through the pillow.

"Who does darling?" a soft voice startles him from across the room.
James quickly looks from under his pillow at his wife's pale curious face.

"No one darling," he lies, "how are you feeling this morning?"

"Like you're hiding something from me," she replies, "now please answer my question."

"I'm thinking of penning an autobiography," he lies to her, "you know a chance to reflect back on all my memoirs and achievements, most notably marrying you Jessica."

Mrs. Jessica Radicon is thirty-six years old and has loved James Radicon since the moment she laid eyes on him.

She knew he was richer than God when they first started dating, but that didn't matter she never wanted his money. He was worth much more to her than material possessions, cash, and an eternally glamorous lifestyle. To her, he was her soul mate.

Jessica's gray eyes are clear and wise. Her strawberry blonde hair is much more strawberry than it ever was blonde. She's a natural red head, but she started tinting her hair with blond highlights a few years back to liven up her appearance. Now that Jessica is getting older, although she is still quite stunning herself, she's sure her husband's handsome eyes are going to begin to wonder soon.

She always suspected he might be cheating, but she's well aware that the life he has afforded her would never have been possible without him. Before they were married she insisted they sign a prenuptial agreement just to prove that she wasn't there for his money. She really wasn't, and she would love him just the same if he was homeless.

"Your memoirs huh..." she says.

"Yes baby," he lies again jumping out of bed to approach her, "Jess you know there's only one woman for me." He kisses her softly on the forehead and then makes his way to the bathroom.

After closing and locking the bathroom door behind him. James pulls his cell phone out of his pocket. He quickly texts her back and then places his phone back safely in the pocket of his Polo sweat pants.

Next he grabs his tooth brush and begins looking for his favorite Crest toothpaste. He looks around all three sinks on the top of his beautiful marble bathroom counter top. He can't find a tube of toothpaste anywhere.

He opens the medicine cabinet to his right. He sees every possible pill and ointment for any ailment or disease imaginable, but absolutely no Crest toothpaste. One by one he opens each of the five drawers going down the front of the sink. No Crest toothpaste.

"Oh damn it, that's right. She threw it all away." he whispers to himself.

In the very back corner on the right side of the black marble sink top, he sees a transparent blue bottle baring the words, "Blue Tooth Technology" and the name Dr. Gregory Blue. Jessica was watching some late night infomercial about some crazy dentist out in Waco Texas who invented some kind of miracle salve that is supposed to replace your regular tooth paste and mouth wash, strengthen your teeth and gums, and restore your teeth to their most healthy form.

James shakes his head silently. Holding his yellow Crest tooth brush beneath the dispenser he pushes its top down to release the miracle goo. The weird watery concoction immediately begins to spill out on and around his toothbrush and on the sink-top.

After each bristle is covered James prepares himself for how bad this stuff just might taste. He would turn on the sink and wet his toothbrush first, but Dr. Blue's goo has wet the brush quite enough already.

As he puts the brush in his mouth and begins to brush, amazingly the taste of the salve isn't bad at all. In fact, it tastes like fresh fruit, and it's foaming up nicely prompting James to brush more thoroughly than he normally would. He can definitely feel the salve working fiercely through his mouth. Jessica may not have made a mistake with this particular purchase, he thinks to himself.

After rinsing his fresh mouth out, James strips down completely naked and jumps in the shower turning it on full blast. As he lathers his towel with some ridiculously expensive West African soap Jessica bought and insists he uses, James is mentally preparing himself for the day he has ahead of him at the office.

After placing the black bar of soap back in its crystal dish on the side of the shower he begins to rub his body thoroughly with the soapy towel. As his hands glide across his chiseled white body, he's imagining his hands are Carolyn's hands. She's taking immense pleasure in exploring every inch of his body.

From his strong neck, to his tense broad shoulders, all the way down to his ripped abdomen. As her hands caress his back with the soft towel she notices his sudden arousal. She takes hold of him as he throbs fiercely in the palm of her hand.

James smiles to himself as he realizes his imagination was never this vivid before he met Carolyn Olivier. Her hands feel so soft on his strong pulsating penis.

As she begins to stroke him masterfully he leans back against the side wall of the shower. Her strokes are becoming more intense as he rises up on the tips of his toes balancing himself with one stable hand on the glass shower door in front of him.

His throbbing member feels huge and powerful in her hands; it's almost too much for her to stroke. She begins to use both hands. He can't take much more of this; the speed at which she can force him to climax is unreal. Just the thought of her is an insanely powerful aphrodisiac for him. Up even higher on the tips of his toes now stroking himself full force James' entire body grows extremely tense.

"Oh Carolyn..." he moans as he spills his seed forth all over the glass shower doors. As he watches his semen squirt out all over the glass he can barely contain himself. He wants to scream her name out, but he thinks better of it realizing his wife Jessica is right outside the bathroom reading a book.

After lazily toweling himself off sitting on his gorgeous immaculate marble toilet, James slides into a pair of cocaine white Polo boxer briefs. With his yellow towel secured around his neck he opens the bathroom door and makes his way back to his enormous bed.

Sitting on the edge of the side of his bed just across from Jessica's reading chair James stares over at her. She feels his eyes on her but she doesn't look up at him. Lost in a trance Radicon begins to think to himself...

Where did I go wrong? I'm a good, strong, white, Christian man. I'm handsome, intelligent, more than affluent... hell I live in my very own mansion. I have a wife who loves me there is no doubt about that. But is she still enough... obviously not. As a man, as a good white Christian man the last thing I want to do is embarrass and rip apart my family by getting caught being unfaithful to my wife Jessica. Damn it we said real vows... and bound our hearts and lives together sixteen years ago. We have two gorgeous children, a son Lucas 16, and a daughter Katherine she's 15. If their friends, my friends, or my wife's friends ever found out what I was doing with Carolyn they would never understand or forgive me. So in turn I must stop the madness now. I'm going to fire her today and rid my life of her disruptive black ass forever.

James' clothes are laid out on the bed perfectly. For some reason today he's noticing all the things he usually doesn't. This woman, his wife works very hard to make, and keep his life as simple as humanly possible.

For years he's felt as if after finishing his morning shower his outfit for the day has just always magically appeared towards the foot of the bed, always in the very same spot. But it was never magic. It was the carefully thought out love and dedication of his wife Jessica.

As he puts his clothes on he glances at his rose gold MK watch. He's late. James throws on his suit as quickly as he can, kisses Jessica softly on the lips, and then storms out of their room and all the way down stairs.

The tasty aroma of pancakes, scrambled eggs, and bacon could be smelled all the way upstairs in the master bedroom. Without much time to eat James grabs a plate and a fork on his way out of the door.

"Hey Dad..." his son Lucas Radicon calls out to him wearing white Ray Ban sunglasses with clear lenses, a baby blue neatly tucked in Polo shirt with a pink logo, white Polo shorts with a baby blue logo, and pink and white Polo shoes. James looks at his teenage son for a moment, and then heads out of the door as if he hadn't said a word to him.

As James drives off in his black on black 2015 Mercedes Benz coupe he ponders why he never deals with any of his family issues head on. He wonders if he's afraid or if maybe he's just not capable of dealing with these sensitive issues appropriately. If there's a problem at one of his many businesses, he's right on it.

He listens to the problem, weighs out his options carefully, and then executes the best possible course of action to resolve said problem. But when it comes to his family he always closes the door and blocks their problems out until he can make himself believe he's forgotten all about whatever the issue was.

Thirty minutes later Mr. Radicon pulls up to the large building that houses his main company, the gorgeous Radicon Winery. James has his hands in hundreds of successful business ventures, but his winery is the one he is the most passionate about.

The great Radicon Winery sits on 7.5 acres of land. The majority of the land is covered in grapevines. Grape growing is both simple and confounding. While it is easy to keep a grapevine alive it is one of agriculture's great difficulties to continue to produce grapes of good enough quality to produce a fine wine. Radicon Winery boasts some of the tastiest wines in not only the U.S. but the entire world.

The building that sits at the very center of the largish vineyard is where the business side of the winery is handled. James has hundreds of offices from corner to corner of the five story structure. These offices are inhabited by his many sales reps, marketing execs, and other various employees that help his company run smoothly from day to day.

Carolyn Olivier started working at the winery two years ago as a field laborer in the vineyard. Five days a week she and her 200 plus coworkers would all go out into the vineyard and tend to the grounds.

Some were equipped with backpack sprayers that they used to spray the vines to keep them pest and disease free. Others trimmed the vines, took care of pesky weeds, and even mowed the lawn around and in between the vines.

Carolyn though was a grape picker. James knows countless other top notch Vineyard owners use mechanical harvesters to pick their grapes, but he likes the old fashion way much better. When he tastes a glass of his wine he wants to know that some hardworking soul took time to carefully pick each one of the delicious grapes he's drinking with love and purpose.

Carolyn wasn't too fond of her job in the vineyard, but she never once complained. She needed the money for her family and the pay wasn't bad at all.

James still remembers the day he met Carolyn Olivier like it was just yesterday. It was about 14 months ago. He was riding through the vineyard in one of his personal golf carts when out of the corner of his eye he saw a woman bending over displaying her round, perfect, voluptuous behind. He stopped his cart immediately, got off and began walking calmly in her direction.

On his way to her he divisively engaged in a couple meaningless conversations with some of his other vineyard employees as not to make his current mission to obvious. By the time he reached her she was standing up right again carefully picking each grape in her section one by one.

Standing not far behind her James cleared his throat and said, "I think you missed one." Carolyn immediately threw her bucket down to the ground and spun around to him with a venomous scowl on her face.

"Listen wise ass," she said, "I don't know who you think you are, but I work very hard in this damn vineyard. I don't bother anybody; I don't gripe or complain I just work damn hard. So if you think your little comment was funny... Then you can just kiss my black ass." James smiled at her sassiness as she bent down to recapture her large grape bucket.

"I'd love too." he replied. She spun around to him again refusing to acknowledge his unmistakably white teeth, his bright light blue eyes, and his radiant smile. "Excuse me," she said, "you would love to what... Kiss my black ass?"

"Why yes ma'am." he said through that perfect smile. "I am a married woman," the 22-year-old Carolyn told him, "and this is sexual harassment. If you don't turn around and leave now I'm going to be forced to march right up to the main building and tell Mr. Radicon about your behavior." "Well is that so?" James asked Carolyn in animated amusement.

Just then a white gentleman approached the two of them. "Mr. Radicon," he said, "your wife left a message for you to call home... It's about your son Lucas."

"Okay Brad I'll call her." Radicon said shaking the man's hand just before he turned to leave.

Carolyn at that point had dropped her grape bucket again and was covering her mouth with both hands in total embarrassment. James smiled at her and extended his hand in her direction. "It's nice to meet you... my name is James Radicon, and what's your name?" he asked in a charming tone.

"I am so sorry Mr. Radicon, I had no idea it was you... Well that you were him or you... Oh damn it I'm sorry." she said laughing at herself as she shook his large hand.

They exchanged phone numbers and a week later Carolyn had a job inside the main building. James couldn't help but feel like their situation was reminiscent of a slave and her master 300 to 400 years ago, but this fact for some reason enticed his unorthodox mind even more.

"Good morning Mr. Radicon." a familiar voice says from the door of his office snatching him away from his daydream. He looks up to see her. She's wearing a gorgeous yellow pant suit and black heels. She knows yellow is his favorite color.

Her naturally curly hair is pulled up into a tight neat bun on top of her head. Her yellow blazer is open just enough to playfully expose the top of her perky bosom. James is trying to ignore how pretty she is because his plan is to fire her this morning.

"I brought your doughnuts and tea sir that you asked me for..." she tells him.

"Doughnuts and tea..." he says.

"Yes sir," she replies, "You know the ones you asked for in your text this morning." she smiles.

He doesn't respond. "Is there anything else you need me to do before I head to my office and begin work on the Brown & Nielsen project?" she asks trying to accurately read his mood.

He remains silent. "Are you okay... James?" she asks closing his door behind her and stepping towards him.

Standing over him now, as he holds his head down in his large hands she puts a soft hand on his left shoulder.

De'Lure

James looks up into her caring hazel eyes.

"Carolyn," he says, "I have to... Tell you something."

"Anything," she kneels down in front of him, "baby you can tell me anything."

Holding her angelic caramel face in between his milky white hands he says, "I have to tell you... You are... an absolutely gorgeous woman." Pulling her into his chest he kisses her long and passionately on her full lips.

(Later that afternoon)

"Come on Ralph Jr., it's time to go baby..." Carolyn calls out from near the front door holding her younger son Karan in her arms tightly.

"Cooooooming mommy." He says running into the front room with one shoe on and the other in his left hand.

Carolyn smiles down at his wide eyes.

"Now I just knew you would beat me to the door little boy," she says, "You told me you wanted mommy to play with you and your baby brother and spend more time with you. Now I cleared my entire schedule for the rest of the day just to take you two to..."

"Chuck E. Cheese!!" Ralph Jr. screams vibrantly.

"Chuckuh Cheese!!" his lovable baby brother tries to mimic him.

"That's right," she smiles opening the front door, "now let's get you both strapped in so we can head over there before it gets too crowded."

Karan nods his adorable little head up and down as his mother walks him to the car in her arms.

"Mommy," Ralph Jr. says walking a step behind her, "Is daddy coming too?"

"Daada, Daada." Karan whines.

"Of course your father is coming." she replies placing Karan down on his feet so she can open the door.

After securing both of her sons in the backseat Carolyn hops in the front seat and straps her seatbelt on just before cranking up her car.
"Conquerors mommy, play conquerors..." Ralph Jr. says from the back seat.

Carolyn smiles as she shakes her head and turns her radio on.

"Please mama..." Her older son begs.

"Please… please." Karan joins in with the begging onslaught.

"I'm trying to find it children," she placates them as she searches her phone, "mama is happy ya'll's favorite song is a gospel song, and I'll play it as many times as your tiny ears wanna hear it."

She finds the song and presses play as she backs out of her long driveway.

"It was your favorite song first mommy." Ralph Jr. says.

"That's right," she confirms, "when mommy was a little girl she used to always lead this song in the youth choir."

"What's a lead mommy?" Ralph Jr. asks playing with his baby brother's toes.

"A lead," Carolyn says, "or a leader is the person everyone else looks up to or follows."

"I wanna be a leader mommy." Ralph Jr. proclaims.

"Well," she smiles at him in her rearview mirror, "If you're anything like your mommy, you will be a leader one-day baby boy."

"Is daddy a leader mommy?" Ralph Jr. asks.

"Daada..." his baby brother smiles.

"Your father," Carolyn hesitates, "is... the leader of our household. Every man should be the leader of his house baby."

"But mommy," Ralph Jr. whines, "you said a leader was the person everyone is posed to look up to and follow. Daddy looks up to you, mommy."

"Where on earth did you come from child?" Carolyn smiles at her remarkably attentive son.

As they pull into the parking lot of Chuck E. Cheese Carolyn pulls out her cell phone to call her husband. As she pulls into an open space near the front the phone is still ringing. She steps out of the car, hangs up, and tries to call again. No answer. With the phone to her ear calling a third time Carolyn opens the backdoor to get her children out of the car.

Once inside Karan follows his big brother towards a racing game. Carolyn watches them both carefully with a distant smile painted on her tired face.

"Come on Ralph answer the phone," she mumbles, "we agreed to meet here and spend time with the kids together for once."

Carolyn hangs up again and slips her phone in her purse as her sons' rush towards her carrying the two powerful smiles that always seem to wash all her pain away.

"Boys," she says looking down at the two of them huddled between her legs, "mommy knows she doesn't spend a lot of time with ya'll right now but I will always be your mama and I'll never let anything bad happen to you. I love you both very much."

"Okay," Ralph Jr. smiles, "can we have pizza now mommy?"

"Pissa, pissa!!" Karan squeals.

"I'll take that as a **we love you too** mommy," Carolyn smiles as a lone tear streams down the left side of her beautiful face, "and yes ya'll go play mama will go get you a pizza."

Ch. 3
"The Brown & Nielsen Project"

Patrick Brown and Renaldo Nielsen are the joint owners of the Los Angeles based "Brown & Nielsen" Winery. The last few years have not been very good to them.

After researching their company and their decline in sales over the past three years, Carolyn reached out to Mr. Brown himself via email to discuss the possibility of merging his company with Radicon's Winery or just selling his winery to Mr. Radicon outright. For about six months he played hard ball, but just last week Carolyn got a call from Mr. Brown's partner Renaldo Nielsen saying he was interested in selling his half of the company to Radicon. His only stipulation was that he wanted to meet James in person in California.

James looks up from his desk to see Carolyn standing just outside of his office door speaking to a handsome, young, biracial kid named Justin Tolls. James knows the young man's name well. He actually hired Justin on at the winery full time himself recently.

Justin is a standout student in the School of Business Administration at the local University of Miami. He interned at the Radicon Winery for three months, and just last week James called him into his office to hire him on full time. But if he's sweet on Ms. Carolyn Olivier, his tenure at this particular Winery may be cut a little short.

Carolyn finishes her obviously delightful conversation with Justin, shakes his hand a little longer than James thinks she should have, and then she looks through his door at James. Her heart quickly sinks to her stomach. His gaze and its meaning are definite.

He's not happy with her.

She looks down at her shoes knowing her face must be red with fear, and confusion. She straightens her long pink dress and knocks politely on his thick office door.

He spins his expensive office chair around to face in the opposite direction from where she's standing. She walks in his office anyway. "James..." she speaks. He doesn't respond. "I uh... Spoke to Mr. Renaldo Nielsen in California." she tells him.

Radicon spins back around to face her.

"Well come on with it," he says, "what did the old fool say?"

"He wants to sell." she says.

"Finally," James flashes a greedy smile, "Cheer up girl this is great news!"

"Not quite." she replies.

"What do you mean not quite," he asks, "of course this is good news... all of it. If I can get the controlling share of the "Brown & Nielsen Winery" I can expand my brand and my genius methods all across the West Coast."

Carolyn looks down again. James stands up from his chair, his face and neck turning bright red now.

"Damn it bitch, speak," he fumes, "what is this? What the hell is all of that looking down at your feet crap? Women are such weak pitiful creatures, especially you, black ones. What in God's name is wrong with you now?"

She looks up at him. "You hate to travel sir." she mumbles.

"Damn it, speak up," he growls, "I can't understand you people... You, you... All of you speak too fast and you don't form your damn words."

"You hate to travel." she repeats a little louder this time.

"I don't speak Ebonics," he tells her, "you people just make up your own damned words and just form sentences however you damn well please. Ignorant, it's just stupid..."

"Damn it James," she interjects throwing her paperwork down on his floor, "I said you hate to travel. I said each word very clearly. I pronounced and enunciated each word perfectly. Your speech on the other hand leaves much to be desired.

"And what the hell is wrong with the way I talk?" he asks.

"You always sound like you're drunk, angry, chewin' tobacco, and on your way to shoot a damn deer." she playfully mocks his deep southern drawl.

"And then at times," she continues, "you sound like an English college professor. I have no clue who you are sometimes. Which one are you James Radicon, a rich southern hick... Or an arrogant affluent Floridian businessman? Or both?" she laughs again.

Unable to keep a straight face for long, James soon joins his gorgeous employee in her jubilant laughter at his expense.

"**God**, Carolyn your laugh is just... its life to me." he tells her. She blushes.

"Well thank you, sir I guess," she replies bending down to retrieve the papers she threw on his floor, "but as I was saying; I know you hate to travel, but the only way Nielsen will agree to sell his share of the company to you is if you fly out to Los Angeles and meet him in person... **Next week**."

James' pleasant smile fades instantly.

"Out of the question." he sits back down in his chair.

"But sir..." she starts.

"There are no buts, girl," he growls, "You know I hate to travel."

"Well yes sir I know, but..." she tries to finish her statement again.

"I am not getting on an airplane Carolyn not now, not ever." he interjects. "But why not James," she asks, "you have all this damn money and now you're faced with the opportunity to at least triple your fortune, but you are scared to fly. Why?"

Radicon spins his chair away from her to face the back wall of his office. "My father," he starts, "Raymond Radicon got on a plane one day 26 years ago and I never saw him again."

"Oh my God," Carolyn gasps covering her full lips with her left hand, "the plane James, whatever happened to the plane?" "It was never found, and neither was my father." he tells her.

Carolyn walks over to close and lock his office door. Then she carefully closes all of his blinds so no one can possibly see inside of his office.

With both hands she pulls the straps of her long dress over her shoulders and lets it fall to the floor. Standing there in a matching white lace bra and panty set, she reaches up to undo her bun. After shaking her heads to release all of her glorious curls she speaks.

"I'm sorry about your father James," she says, "but I will not let you miss out on this deal that I worked so hard to land for you. You are going to California next week..."

He stands up quickly from his chair and then turns around to face her.

"Damn it I said..." his words get caught in his red throat as he stares at her perfect seminude body.

"You're going James," she tells him, "and I'm going with you."

"Hell yes you are." he rushes towards her.

As he reaches her she jumps into his massive arms wrapping her anxious legs around him. Her sexy caramel skin looks gorgeous next to his almost tan white skin.

He begins to kiss her ever so passionately gripping her round soft behind never closing his eyes. As they stare into each other's knowing eyes they continue to hungrily devour each other's mouths.

"Damn it Carolyn," he moans carrying her en route to his huge mahogany desk, "I was going to fire you today."

"For what?" she asks, as she sucks and bites the left side of his thick neck.

"Are you not satisfied with my efforts?" she continues.

"Oh shut up." he smiles down at her.

Then James begins to push everything on his huge desk towards the back of it. Carolyn drops down to her well trained knees and unbuttons his pants, and then rips his zipper open.

He's already more than ready for her. She masterfully grabs hold of his enormous member. Licking the sides of it she strokes him softly with both hands.

"Not today..." he moans. He grabs her by her hair forcing her to stand up straight. Then he picks her up and sits her on top of his desk. Radicon takes a few steps back to admire his Nubian queen. With her heels down flat on his desktop she has her legs spread wide for him.

James throws his luxurious blazer on the floor and then button by button he opens his Polo dress shirt exposing his rock hard six pack. Pulling his undershirt up, he unveils the perfect V-cut above his private area. She loves his V-cut; it gets her wetter than anything else.

She can feel her breathing pattern changing rapidly. She can no longer contain herself; she needs James Radicon inside her right this instant.

As he approaches her she quickly takes off her passion soaked underwear. He stopped using condoms with her months ago. He puts the head in, struggling to get all of him inside of her small frame.

It always feels like the first time when they're together. If only either one of their marriages could feel the same way, they wouldn't be locked in this office screwing each other's brains out right now.

Yes. He finally breaks through again. He runs his long, strong, penis as deep inside her as she will let it go. She closes her eyes as she bites her quivering bottom lip. "James..." she cries.

"Open your eyes Carolyn," he whispers, "I want to stare at your soul while I fuck you. Look at me... ***Every fiber of your being belongs to me... forever.***"

De'Lure

She stares back at him obediently. Carolyn's passion filled screams and moans are growing louder with each powerful stroke. James reaches over and grabs her panties. "Open your mouth." he demands. She obeys. Then he stuffs her wet panties in her unsuspecting mouth. "Don't take your eyes off of me..." he moans. She obeys between her muffled screams.

His blue eyes are hypnotizing her as he strokes harder and deeper inside of her cum drenched center. "You are one of my most prized possessions..." he moans.

"I'm all yours James..." she mumbles through her tasty wet panties.

"Passion Absolute"

I COULD SNATCH DOWN EVERY SINGLE STAR FROM THE SKY

THEN PAINT THEM DELICATELY BENEATH YA FEET

JUST SO I COULD WATCH YOU FLY

I SEE STARDUST WHEN YOU TAKE OFF BUT I'M RIGHT BEHIND YOU

I NEVER MIND TOO

CUZ THE ONLY TIME MY MIND IN TUNE WIT HEART IS WHEN I FIND YOU

NOW NEVER MIND THE TUNES I COULD DO ANIME OR MUSIC TOO

MY TALENT IS ON A SWIVEL I CAN CREATE ANYTHING I DREAM TO

BUT MUSIC IS THE SOUNDTRACK OF OUR LIVES THIS IS TRUE

AND THERE ARE NO LIES BETWEEN OUR EYES WE HAVE A PASSION ABSOLUTE

IF YOU NEVER HAD A CLUE WHAT LOVE COULD DO

I COULD SHOW YOU PASSION BLUE

AND EVERY OTHER HUE OF TRUE LOVE THERE'S MORE THAN JUST A FEW

LIKE HEARTBREAK PURPLE

FEELING THIS IS CERTAIN JUST DON'T GO IN CIRCLES

OR LONG LASTING LAVENDER

THAT'S THE ONE YOU SHOULD MARRY HER

OR BREAK DOWN BROWN WHEN YOUR HEART POUNDS

AND YOU DECIDE TO DROWN

IN BUCKETS AND OCEANS OF SORROW

SEE ORANGE IS FOR NEW FLAME

NOT THE LIES THAT YOU CLAIM

IF YOU CAN POWER THROUGH THE PAIN YOU'LL FIND CHANGE

BUT AS FOR MY BOO

EVERY STEP I'LL EVER TAKE IS WALKIN CLOSER TO YOU

AND WHEN I'M LOOKIN THROUGH YA WINDOWS

AND IM TALKIN BOUT YA EYES

I CAN SEE YA SOUL AND THAT'S WHERE MY HEART LIES

AND IF I EVER LIE TO YOU THAT LIE WOULD CLAIM TRUE

THAT I COULD TAKE ANY OTHER WOMAN ON THE PLANET

AND MAKE HER JUST LIKE YOU

BUT SEE THAT WOULD BE A PAINFUL CYCLE FOR MICHAEL

TO TRY TO PSYCHE HER UP TO BE AN ANGELIC IDOL TOO

BABE I ONLY GOT EYES FOR YOU

HEAVEN IS MY LIMIT I'M ONLY SKYIN' FOR YOU

AND I'MA KEEP FLYING TILL MY NAME IS THE TRUTH

PAIN PRODUCES PASSION MY BRAIN IS PROOF

EVEN DEEP INSIDE THAT CAGE ALL I HAD WAS TRUTH

NOW I'M FREE AS A BIRD DOIN WHAT MASTERS DO

I COULD BE SINGLE FOREVER JUST LIKE BACHELORS DO... BUT

*I'D RATHER HOLD YO HAND FOREVER AND BREAK OUR
HEARTS IN TWO*

SO THEY COULD BEAT FOREVER LIKE HEARTS IN TANDUM DO

A PASSION ABSOLUTE

"MY PRAYER"

I pray that you all love and enjoy my characters as well as their stories. Know that all things are possible through Christ who strengthens us, and we can do nothing that matters without Him.

In Jesus name I pray Amen.

M. De'Lure

About the Author

De'Lure is a dreamer who writes with his heart and a very realistic imagination. His first passion was acting, but from that love spawned an even deeper passion for the art of writing. The imagery he uses to create stories is packed with all the components of legendary writing careers. Expect great things from De'Lure.

If you enjoyed this novel you should check out these other *AMAZING* titles by De'Lure

Onyx Cielo: Book 1 -The Tree of Transformation- (Fantasy)

Take My Breath Away: Orlando Nights – RELOADED- (Realistic Romance/ Drama)

Take My Breath Away 2: When Love Calls (Realistic Romance/ Drama)

Take My Breath Away 3: Save me from my Past (Realistic Romance/ Drama)

Passion Absolute –Radicon's Princess- (Realistic Romance/ Drama/Erotica)

De'Lure Shorts & Poem (Poetry/Drama/Short Stories)

He Without Sin (Realistic/Romance/Drama)

The Art of Beauty (Realistic/ Island Romance/ Drama)

Mental Apex (Poetry)

Kissed (Murder Mystery/Suspense/ Romance)

Available through Infinitypublishing.com, Outskirtspress.com, Amazon.com, Barnes&noble.com, and many other retailers. Signed copies can also be ordered directly from the author.

Email: ceom.love@gmail.com
FB: Published De'Lure

www.ingramcontent.com/pod-product-compliance
Lightning Source LLC
Chambersburg PA
CBHW072228190626
46809CB00017B/1529